The White Ghost and Temple of Seven Seas

Nia Arteniani

The author of this story is a student majoring in astrophysics, at the University of Massachusetts Amherst, USA. From age 10, she dreamed about fantastic stories with unusual worlds, about multiverses and people with superpowers. The author's real dream is at the heart of this story. You will experience a fantastic world of fantasy and adventure. Happy reading everyone!

PART I: The Prophecy Begins

Prologue: The Nature of Heroes

Everyone wants to be a superhero—doing good deeds by punishing evil. Our world just can't live without heroes. They are our lifeguards, our policemen, the guardians of our souls. They stand between us and the darkness, carrying a burden we are too afraid—or too weak—to carry ourselves.

But wait…

Has anyone ever wondered about their lives? Did anyone ask who they are, what they feel, whether they need saving too? No…

We clap, we cheer, we call their names in times of danger, but when the danger passes, we forget them. Heroes are often left alone with their fears, their sacrifices, their hidden scars. Everyone waits for miracles, hoping they will happen as if by divine will.

But who are the heroes, really? Perhaps they are not chosen by the gods at all. Perhaps they are ordinary people—like you and me—who chose to rise when others fell, who decided to fight when it would have been easier to run. Perhaps they are people who refused to accept the world as it was, and in that refusal, became something more.

And so, the truth is simple: we can be heroes too. All it takes is a wish. A decision. An effort. And everything can turn out differently than it was written. In our world, we can do anything. Right?

Let us begin with the story of one such girl, a legend whispered by sailors, sung in taverns, and etched in the memory of kingdoms. Some called her the White Ghost, others the Daughter of the Seas, but in her homeland she was simply Nika.

Her story begins in Syracuse, Greece, in a marble palace overlooking the Aegean. The king and queen had a daughter, Nicoleta. She was smart, kind, endlessly curious, and possessed of a restless courage that set her apart from childhood. The maids, enchanted by her spirit, called her Nika, in honor of the ancient Greek goddess of victory. For she did indeed love to win, whether it was in games, debates, or the endless contests she invented against herself. Over time, the name Nicoleta was forgotten, and everyone knew her as Nika.

She grew up quickly, becoming more beautiful and wiser with every passing season. Hours of her days were devoted to the palace library, a vast collection of scrolls and manuscripts gathered from all corners of the known world. She read of gods and heroes, of lost civilizations, of great wars and greater reconciliations. She read about the Seven Seas, about distant lands where elephants roamed and dragons still whispered beneath mountains. Knowledge became her greatest treasure, and wisdom her shield.

Yet Nika was not content to remain cloistered among books and marble columns. As the future queen, she believed it was her duty to know her people, to see them not through reports but with her own eyes. Once a week, she would slip away from the palace gates, flanked by guards but walking with a simple cloak, observing the lives of her citizens. She would linger at the market stalls, watching fishermen mend their nets, potters shape clay, and children chase one another barefoot through the dust. She noticed the smallest details—the way a mother's hands trembled as she counted her last coins for bread, or the quiet pride of a farmer displaying his harvest.

"Why only once a week?" she often asked her father.

And the king would answer with stern finality: "Because the world beyond these walls is dangerous. A princess belongs in the palace, not in the streets."

But Nika's heart longed for the freedom of those streets. She envied the laughter of children who played without care, the boldness of sailors who returned from storms, and even the merchants whose lives were uncertain but full of movement.

Once or twice a month, when the merchant ships arrived in the harbor, the city would transform. The docks filled with shouts and song, with scents of exotic spices, leather, and tar. People gathered to buy cloth from the East, wine from Italy, ivory from Africa. Nika would beg her guards to let her mingle, and for a fleeting hour she felt almost like one of them—an ordinary girl among ordinary people, marveling at the wonders of the world.

Yet even then, destiny seemed to trail her like a shadow. Old women would grasp her hand and whisper blessings. Strangers looked at her with a strange recognition, as though they saw in her something she did not yet see in herself.

Nika did not know it then, but the path of a hero was already unfolding.

Chapter 1: The Pirate Game

One day, Nika wanted to see the new goods. She hurried to the harbor, finding a large crowd. The guard ordered everyone to let the princess pass. She approached one of the merchants.

"Your Highness, this is a wonderful wooden chest. Would you like it? It costs only 40 drachmas," said the merchant.

The princess declined and asked, "Where do you get such beautiful things, and why don't pirates attack you?"

"They do attack, Your Highness. Last time, they stole many goods, but today's sale was successful. We bring goods from Rome, India, and other Eastern countries," the merchant replied.

"Isn't it expensive for the villagers?" asked the princess.

"Our work is highly valued; these things are difficult to obtain."

"Why can't you defend yourselves against pirates?"

"They are strong and ruthless," the merchant said.

Satisfied with her curiosity, she ran to the beach. She loved the sea—it was inspiring and amazing. As she admired the view, three boys played nearby. Suddenly, one boy accidentally pushed Nika, and they both fell into the water.

"Are you alright?" one boy asked.

"Not quite."

"Alex, are you blind? You're talking to the princess! Apologize immediately!" said another boy.

"I didn't know. Sorry, Your Highness."

"Don't call me that. I'm outside the castle. Call me by my name."

"And what is your name?"

"Nika—just Nika."

"Very nice. I'm Alex, this is my brother Ios, and my friend Lucas. We're playing as pirates."

"What do you like about them?" Nika asked.

"They're cool, strong, free, and masters of the oceans!"

"But they rob and kill innocent people. That's not good."

"Yes, but they're very rich," Lucas said.

"Do they help anyone?"

"Of course not," Alex laughed.

Nika looked upset.

"Would you like to be a pirate?" Nika asked.

"Yes!" the boys shouted.

"Can I also be a pirate?"

"No way. Girls aren't allowed on ships; it's bad luck," said Ios.

"They're not suited for the sea," added Lucas.

"Can I at least play with you?"

"Yes, here is a stick."

Nika took the stick and began fencing with Alex. She had learned swordsmanship since childhood. With one move, she disarmed him.

"This is fun."

"How did you do that?" Alex was surprised.

"I've read about fencing and know different moves."

"Will you teach us?" Ios asked.

"Yes, but later," Nika said, running off without explanation.

The next day, Nika disguised herself in her father's clothes and escaped the palace. She met the boys again, and they began a friendship that would shape their futures. Together, they shared adventures, challenges, and secrets that would define the legend of the White Ghost.

Running to the beach, Nika tried to find yesterday's boys, but no one was there. Disappointed, she sat down in the sand. It took about 10 minutes, as in the distance she heard voices coming from a distance. The boys were walking towards the shore, laughing out loud and talking to each other. Nika quickly jumped up and ran to them.

"Hello guys, can I play with you today?"

"Who are you?"

"You don't recognize me?" she replied.

"Not?!" Said Alex.

"It's me Nika, the princess. I just put on my dad's clothes to escape from the palace."

"Nika, is that really you?"

"Yes."

The boys were surprised at first, but then they began to get used to her new look. Now she was like them, --bold, daring and always ready for a fight. She taught them swordsmanship as she promised. Then Nika told them her plans for the future, how much she wants to travel herself, helping people and animals.

Lucas said that her plans will not work. Nika asked, "Why not?"

"Because you have to be a queen in order to govern the whole kingdom."

Nika fell silent, lost in thought.

The day passed quickly, and darkness fell. Nika suddenly realized her parents were probably looking for her. She was about to run back to the palace when a boat moored to the shore nearby. Two strangers pulled a bound dophin from it. He was still alive. His body fought desperately, hoping to free himself. Men pulled out knives, and they wanted to kill a dolphin ...

"Stop, do not dare, I order you!" Nika voice rang out, sharp and frantic.

Nika's heart was pounding wildly.

"You heard that, John, we have a little brat givin' orders."

"Get lost before you regret it," snarled one of the pirates.

"It's none of your business," added another.

"I order you to release the dolphin immediately, otherwise…" And here Nika faltered.

"Otherwise, what?" The pirates began to laugh.

In a flash, Nika grabbed the first stone that came across and launched into one of the pirates. Yes, the stone struck him straight on the head. He yelped in surprise and pain.

"John, catch this brat." He ran after Nika.

Everything happened very quickly. John grabbed Nika by his arm, but she twisted free and kicked sharply to his shin. And while he pulled out a knife from his belt, Nika seized a wooden stick and struck him hard across his back. John winced in pain. She, took advantage of the moment and ran to the boat. Second pirate rushed at Nika with a knife and while she was dodging from the first one, the boys ran to her aid and began beating him with sticks. The pirate had no choice but to take off running leaving his unconscious friend behind. Nika took the knife that the pirate dropped and cut the dolphin's ropes. He was free but he was too weak and could not jump into the water himself. The children had to push the dolphin towards the water.

"What happened? Why aren't you swimming?" asked Nika.

"Thanks a lot! I will never forget your kindness" said dolphin in human voice.

Nika gasped in surprise.

"You… You can talk?" Nika asked in surprise.

"You're special if you can understand me." said dolphin, "I will thank you."

"Will I see you again?" Nika asked.

The dolphin dipped its head and disappeared into the blue sea, leaving Nika staring after it.

"You guys heard, I spoke with a dolphin, he talked to me! And yes, he spoke!" said Nika.

"I don't understand what you're talking about, he just squeaked something and you squeaked back at him." said Lucas.

"I am telling you that I understood him!" said Nika.

"Yeah, yeah but how!?" Alex said.

"Shh, we need to get out of here as soon as possible." said Lucas, looking at the unconscious pirate.

"That's right, that's right." Ios said.

The children ran in different directions.

Nika knew how to get into the palace without being seen she had her own secret way. However, the guards were standing at her secret location and waiting for princess to come back. The guards did not recognize her and grabbed her by her hands, taking her to the king.

"Let me go, I'm a princess, you fools." Nika screamed.

But the guards didn't listen.

"Your Majesty, we caught a rat in palace and he claim to be a princess."

Seeing Nika, the king approached her and, of course, recognized her. He gave the order to the guards to leave. And then asked her in a chilling voice. Where has she been all day?

"What you were doing and how dare you not showing up for dinner." said King.

Chapter 2: The Crystal Dream

"And what, do I have to sit in the palace all the time, without seeing people, the sea, or nature?" Nika demanded.

"You are a princess and it is not right for you to behave like this. You shouldn't risk your life. You are the future heiress of our kingdom. And for Zeus's sake what are you wearing?" the king snapped.

"These are your trousers and your T-shirt. They suit me very well, don't they?"

"Take it off immediately! You will be punished under house arrest."

"So be it, but I want to tell you something that will make you happy." said Nika.

"And what is it?"

"Today I saved a dolphin from the hands of the pirates."

"Very funny!"

"No, it's true, I even talked to him."

"You should grow up already, Nicoleta and stop thinking about silly things."

"Do not call me that. I am Nika, I am victory", she sobbed, then turned and fled to her room.

Nika slept restlessly that night, waking up often as thoughts spun wildly in her head, haunted by emotions and memories. Eventually, she slipped into a deep dream.

The dolphin returned – but now he appeared in human form. A handsome, mysterious figure with sea-glass eyes and hair like sunning sun. He held his hands a glowing crystal shaped with 77 facets, each reflecting light in every color imaginable.

He stretched it toward her. "Now you have it.", he whispered.

Rays of light, from all 77 sides, began to permeate Nika's entire body. She felt mix of coldness and warmth at the same time. For a moment, Nika began to float in the air. Until she sank to the ground and was knocked out of sleep.

Strange, isn't it? Anyways…

A strange feeling seized Nika in the morning; a feeling that something has changed inside her body, although there were no outward signs. Nika got up and walked, but these were not just steps, she instantly teleported to another room and she didn't know how it occurred. Her body felt weightless, her reactions were incredibly fast, and her senses have become sharper.

"What's happening to me?" Nika thought.

On the one hand, this alarmed her, but on the other hand she felt delight and freedom inside.

"What else can I do!?" Nika said to herself.

… But let's not rush!

Still dazed, she joined her parents for breakfast. She wanted to share fer dream but was quickly cut off by her father. He had his own news.

As always!

He said to Nika, that he decided to hire governesses, teachers who will take care of her education. Nika wanted to object to the king, but he was not inclined. Days passed in a haze of lessons. The governesses taught Nika every day, how to playing the piano, etiquette, history, arithmetic and French in general, all sorts of nonsense, as Nika thought. Eventually, she skipped classes altogether.

…But, oh boy, how boring…I know myself.

"I've outgrown them," she told herself. "Why waste time?"

Soon she realized that there was no use in governesses. She decided that it was better to do self-education. She didn't need governesses. She had already surpassed them.

Chapter 3: The Compass

One sunny afternoon, while hiding from another etiquette lesson, Nika wandered into a forgotten wing of the royal library. The air smelled of parchment and salt. As she dusted off shelves, a glint of brass caught her eye—a small, sea-worn compass nestled beneath a pile of scrolls. Oddly, it spun in circles, even without being moved.

Curious, she followed its pull, wandering deeper into the archives until she found a locked cabinet. It gave way with a gentle tug. Inside lay an ancient book, its cover embossed with seven waves and one silver dolphin. The title read: The Temple of the Seven Seas.

Her fingers trembled as she opened it. Symbols danced across the pages—runes she had seen only in dreams. One page shimmered as if alive. It spoke of seven gates, each hidden in a different sea, and a White Ghost who would awaken them. The pages mentioned a prophecy... about a child who could speak with creatures of the deep, and a crystal with 77 sides.

The compass glowed faintly next to the book.

"Why is this here?" Nika whispered. "And why does it feel like it's calling me?"

Just then, footsteps echoed nearby. She slammed the book shut and tucked the compass under her cloak.

This was no ordinary lesson. This was the beginning of something bigger…

…On the way to the king, Nika stopped near the meeting chamber, and an interesting conversation caught her attention. She saw her father and several consuls.

"Father, we need to talk", she said boldly.

"Nicoleta, leave now, now is not the time."

"Your meetings can wait. You're planning taxes and war again, aren't you?"

"Get out of the room. That's an order!"

Nika stepped closer to the table. "I see no reason to attack the coastal port in England. They are not our enemies. If you do this, then England will simply destroy Syracuse. It is better to offer peace with them", she continued.

"And how can we offer peace if they stole our gold?" said one of the consuls.

"Did they? I do not believe that." said Nika loudly and continue:

"Maybe we can meet with the Consul of England and start negotiations."

"Don't be silly, get out of the hall immediately." said King.

"Your Majesty, you daughter said a wise thing, we should pay attention to her words." said one of the consuls.

"If you don't try, you won't know. Right?" Nika continued. "We are also rich. Why do we need another war, Father? To destroy innocent lives?! You're terrible!"

She shook her head and ran into her bedroom.

King was furious at his daughter's behavior.

"Your Majesty, it's a good idea for peace with England, but how?" said another consul.

"I know what to do!" the king exclaimed.

The next day the king called Nika to his cabinet.

"I have good news for you." he said in a chilling voice.

"What news?" Nika said nervously. She already knew something was going to happen. Oh, Zeus and it wasn't good!

"Your classes will continue for another two months."

"What is going to happen after two months?"

"Your wedding."

"What!?" Nika screamed.

"Yes, yes, peace with the Britain through your marriage. You gave us this idea yesterday. Well, done daughter." Father continued in the same calm tone. "You're very helpful for our kingdom."

"No, I did not propose a wedding, only peace with them."

"You're already quite big…"

Nika interrupted her father.

"I want to be free. I want to make my own decisions. I want to be useful to our kingdom, without anyone's help ... Nika wanted to continue her speech, but the king silenced her with a wave of his hand:

"This is your marriage, and it is not discussed, everything was already decided. Maybe this marriage will make you clever."

Chapter 4: The Moment

She ran to her room and quickly began changing clothes.

"I won't let that happen! I will not allow this!" she mumbled, trembling.

In a state of confusion, despair, and horror, Nika felt desperate to talk to someone who would understand her. She needed her only true friends—the three boys from the beach. She ran to the beach frantically began to look for familiar silhouettes with her eyes. Nika ran along the beach side, hoping to see somebody. The shoreline curved, revealing a bay on the horizon. Intuitively Nika ran towards it. And there they were, it can't be, familiar silhouettes approaching her. Nika couldn't believe her eyes.

"Alex, Ios, Lucas, guys!"

"Nika, is that you?"

"What happened? Why are you crying?"

"You look terrified."

Taking a deep breath, she blurted out, "I want to tell you something urgently. This is very important. And I need your help. They want to marry me by force." Nika blurted out.

"Oh, Great Zeus, what are you talking about?" Alex asked incredulously. "Start from the beginning."

Nika launched into a hurried re-telling. They hadn't seen each other in two years. She recounted everything: the dolphin, the dream, the crystal, the compass, the ancient book—and now, the unwanted marriage.

Ios blinked: "You are a princess, and in the future, you will become a queen, maybe it's not such a bad decision after all."

"You're crazy," Nika said angrily. "I don't want to get married against my will, even for the sake of a kingdom."

"Then how are you going to help the country and the people?" asked Lucas.

"I'll find another way, and it seems I already have it."

"And what is it?" asked Alex.

"I will become a pirate."

The boys laughed.

"What's so funny!?"

"Pirates don't do good things, they rob and kill, and live as they want and please."

"And I'll be a different kind of pirate, one the world has not never seen."

"This is a very risky decision."

"You can just die, and besides, how will you escape your father?"

"I can."

"But for that, you will need a ship!"

"I'll buy it."

"You will need sailors!"

"I'll find them."

"And also need knowledge of navigation and languages!"

"I already know it."

"How do you know it?" Lucas exclaimed.

"I skipped the lessons of governesses on purpose, to learn all about astronomy, algebra, navigation, as well I know three languages, know kung fu, and fencing. I hope that is enough for my secret plan."

"Come on, how is it possible to learn all this in 2 years?"

"You're lying to us."

"She's fooling us." said Alex. "We won't listen to her again, she is talking nonsense."

Then Nika ran up to Alex and in an instant, she hooked his legs with her foot and skillfully threw him over her shoulder to the ground. Her right forearm pressed against Alex's throat. He couldn't move, and Nika, looking madly at his eyes, screamed furiously:

"Now, do you believe me? Answer, do you?"

From horror and astonishment boys could not utter a word, what talking about Alex. The pause seemed to be long. Catching her breath and recovering a little, Nika weakened her death grip, and held out hand to Alex.

"I'm sorry, I didn't have a choice how. How would I proved to you that I am telling the truth? I hope everything is fine, Alex?"

A little more time passed, and Alex gradually began to come to his senses. No one expected this from the fragile, gentle, young girl, and even more from a princess.

At the same time boys exclaimed:

"Teach us and we will follow you everywhere and always, we will become your shadow and servants."

They bowed to the princess in recognition and respect for her strength and power.

"No need for bows, I believe you. I will teach you everything that I know myself and we will cross all seas and oceans, we will become stronger than any pirates. We will be the protectors of all people and animals."

"When do we start?" Alex exclaimed, he didn't want to wait to learn the fighting technique that had just demonstrated Nika on him.

"Patience," Nika said, "we will gradually learn all skills and craftsmanship, and also it is important to follow discipline and develop willpower."

Chapter 5: Forging Shadows

For the next two months, Nika became not only a teacher but also a commander, a mentor, and a sister-in-arms to Alex, Ios, and Lucas. Every day they gathered in the cove, away from the eyes of palace guards and curious villagers. It was there, smell of salt spray and pine-scented wind, that their true transformation began.

At dawn, Nika would rouse the boys before the first rays of sunlight touched the cliffs. "Rise," she would command, her voice firm yet encouraging. "Discipline is the seed of strength." They ran along the shoreline until their legs burned, scaling jagged rocks with bare hands to toughen their grip and climbing trees to learn balance. By the time the sun rose fully, their bodies were drenched in sweat, and their lungs burned from the exertion. But their eyes shone with determination.

After the morning trials, Nika led them in martial training. She wielded wooden swords with the precision of a soldier, drilling them in stances, parries, and lunges. Alex, always the fiery one, pushed forward with reckless energy, while Ios showed natural agility and quick reflexes. Lucas struggled at first, his heavy build slowing him down, but his raw strength made him a formidable opponent once Nika taught him patience and control.

But Nika knew that strength of body alone would not make them victorious. She carved sticks into makeshift spears and demonstrated how to throw them with precision. She showed them how to turn ordinary fishing nets into traps, and how to defend themselves with nothing but a staff. When their arms are tired, she taught them breathing exercises she had read about in old Chinese texts, calming their minds and focusing their will.

In the afternoons, the training shifted to knowledge. Sitting on the warm sand, Nika spread out maps and star charts she had secretly copied from the royal library. She taught them the constellations, showing how sailors could find their way across the oceans using the stars alone. With pebbles and shells, she demonstrated the movements of the planets, explaining how tides were governed by the moon. "The sea has its own language," she said, "and if you can learn to read it, it will never betray you."

They also studied languages—Arabic, Latin, and fragments of French. At first the boys resisted, rolling their eyes at memorizing words instead of swinging swords. Like, fight was easier? But when Nika challenged them with coded messages, daring them to decode them before sunset, they took to it with enthusiasm. Slowly, they began to see that knowledge itself was a weapon sharper than any blade. Took them a while to understand it!

The evenings were devoted to unity. They sat around a crackling fire, roasting fish they had caught themselves, sharing stories and laughter. But there was also ritual. Nika had them carve personal emblems into flat stones: Alex chose the lion for courage, Ios the falcon for swiftness, Lucas the bear for strength, and Nika herself the white dolphin, symbol of the sea and the bond she felt with the mysterious creature that had once spoken to her. Together they placed their stones in a circle, swearing loyalty not just to her, but to one another.

Sometimes, when the moon was high, Nika would pull out the compass and the ancient book. The compass needle spun wildly when she opened the book to certain passages, glowing faintly under the starlight. Though the boys could not read the strange runes, Nika felt the words stir in her blood, whispering secrets she is only half-understood. She shared what she could, explaining that their fates were tied not only to Syracuse, but to seas that stretched beyond imagination.

As the days turned into weeks, the cove became their forge. Scrapes healed into scars, voices deepened, and fear gave way to confidence. The boys, once playful children pretending at piracy, were now apprentices of something greater—something they did not yet have a name for. And at the heart of it all was Nika: their leader, their White Ghost, already walking the path of legend.

Chapter 6: The Double Game

BUT...in the palace, another story was unfolding. While her heart burned with rebellion, she wore the mask of obedience.

To her father, she appeared meek, quiet, and submissive. She listened during meals, bowed her head during lectures, and never discussed when governesses tried to correct her even when she was falling asleep during lectures. She even sat politely through endless lessons in etiquette and piano. Everyone thought the princess had finally surrendered to her fate. But it was all a play. A carefully crafted double game.

Nika had learned how to act. Her father saw a daughter who nodded to his every command, while behind closed doors she sharpened blades and planned her escape. At some point, the king thought that how, "can this be true?" "Is it all just a lie?" But he was happy, looking at her changed daughter.

At night, she snuck from her chambers, trading royal silks for rough sailor's clothes, slipping through secret corridors into the city. There, in the shadowed cove with her friends, she trained harder than ever.

The palace prepared for her wedding. Seamstresses stitched gowns heavy with pearls, cooks tested endless banquets, and the king's advisors spoke only of alliances and treaties. But Nika prepared for something else entirely—freedom. She hid daggers beneath her bed, maps under her pillows, and coded notes in the margins of her lesson books.

She learned how to smile when she wanted to scream. She learned how to play her father's game, even as she created her own.

One summer morning, she was woken early by the maids. At breakfast, her father announced in a proud voice that the British prince would soon arrive. "The day draws near," he said, satisfied. "Soon, peace will be sealed by your hand, my daughter."

Nika lowered her eyes and forced a gentle smile. "As you wish, Father," she whispered. Inside, however, her heart pounded like a war drum. She had no intention of being anyone's pawn.

When she was led away to try on her wedding dress, the turquoise gown glittered in the sunlight, covered in diamonds and pearls. The maids gasped at her beauty. Nika stared at her reflection in the mirror, and though she looked every bit the obedient bride, she knew the truth: beneath the silk and gold, she wore her escape clothes, hidden and ready.

The king thought his daughter had finally accepted her destiny. But Nika had already chosen her own.

Chapter 7: The Prince's Arrival

It was a summer morning when the palace stirred earlier than usual. Nika was woken by the servants and informed she must try on her ceremonial dress for the arrival of the British delegation. She dressed obediently, but beneath the gown she wore her traveling clothes, hidden like armor. Her plan was set.

By midday, the carriage of the British consul and Prince Charles arrived at the palace gates. They were welcomed with pomp, banners fluttering in the sea breeze. Inside the throne room, the king and queen greeted them warmly.

"Hello Your Majesty, Hello Your Highness," the prince said, bowing stiffly.

"Welcome, Prince. Glad to see you safe," replied the king.

"And I'm glad too."

"Meet my daughter."

Nika entered, radiant in her turquoise gown glittering with pearls and diamonds. A golden diadem crowned her head. Her beauty stunned the room into silence. But she shattered it with a single word:

"Hi."

Her father, hiding his irritation, left her alone with the prince, hoping he might charm her. "We leave you alone," he said, and the royal court drifted into the gardens.

"What is your name?" Nika asked.

"I am Charles the Thirteenth," the prince replied with a practiced bow.

"Wow, how many Charlese's was before you?" Nika smirked.

"It is our tradition," Charles answered, a touch arrogantly.

Nika's eyes are narrowed. "Why did you take our gold?"

"What?" The prince was started.

"My father told me everything," she pressed.

"We didn't take your gold. You took ours," Charles said bitterly. "To save our country, to avoid dependence. My father agreed to this deal—this marriage—because otherwise there would be war, and we would lose it."

Nika froze, the world tilting beneath her. For years she believed the British were aggressors. But the pain in Charles's voice was too raw to be false, they came from the depths of his heart, saturated with bitterness, pain and despair.

"You know," she said, her voice low but urgent, "I will help you. I will return your gold. Follow me. There's no time to lose."

Charles blinked in shock. "You mean... the vault?"

"Yes. And you're coming with me," Nika replied firmly.

She already knew where the treasure was hidden. The only question was: how to get past the guards?

Chapter 8: Breaking the Chains

And then an idea flashed in her mind. Without hesitation, Nika slipped off her glittering dress, revealing her usual boyish outfit hidden beneath. The silk gown fell to the stone floor like a shed skin. She pointed to it with feigned terror and shouted:

"Guards! The princess is in trouble, save her—she is in danger!"

The guards, started by her panic, rushed into the cellar. The torchlight flickered against the walls, casting long shadows over the vault doors.

"Where? Where is she?" one of them demanded.

"Right there! Quickly!" Nika cried, pointing again at the pile of turquoise silk.

In the twilight glow of the cellar, it was not immediately clear what was happening. Confusion spread, and the guards charged off in search of the imaginary threat, leaving the vault door momentarily unattended.

Seizing the chance, Nika pulled a small key from her pocket. With practiced precision, she unlocked the heavy door and slipped inside. The cold air of the vault wrapped around her as her eyes scanned the chamber. And there it was—ten bags filled to the brim with English gold, their leather sides bulging.

Charles, still pale and trembling, whispered, "But... how can we take them away without anyone noticing? There's not enough time."

Nika's gaze darted to the only window in the room, narrow and barred with iron. Beyond it was nothing but empty air and the jagged cliff face dropping into the sea.

Most would have despaired. Nika smiled. She had a plan.

With a sharp breath, she gripped the bars with both hands, her strength fueled by the crystal's gift. Muscles tensed, stone cracked, and with one violent pull she ripped the iron free, throwing it clattering onto the vault floor. Charles gasped, unable to believe what he was seeing.

Leaning halfway out, Nika tilted her head toward the waves and gave a piercing whistle—an instinctive, ultrasonic call that vibrated deep in her throat. The sound echoed off the cliff walls and carried into the sea.

The water below is stirred. Dark fins sliced the surface. Dolphins.

At once, Nika became a blur of motion, moving back and forth from the bags to the window, lifting sacks twice her size with supernatural speed. She hurled them out one by one, where waiting dolphins caught and balanced them on their sleek bodies, carrying them away toward the British ship anchored offshore.

Charles could only stare from the corner, paralyzed between awe and fear.

When the last bag was gone, Nika turned to him. Her voice rank with command:

"Now, run to your ship. Your gold is already there. Never return to Syracuse, and most importantly—forget everything you saw. Forget me. Now go!"

Charles did not argue. He fled, footsteps echoing into silence.

Nika brushed the dust from her hands, her heart hammering. Then, with fire in her eyes, she raced from the vault and stormed into the ceremonial hall. Her voice rank out like a bell:

"There will be no wedding!"

The hall froze. Every noble, every servant, every guard turned to stare.

Her father's face turned crimson. "What? Where is your dress?"

"I won't wear it!" Nika snapped, standing tall.

"Enough! What antics are these? You shame us before our guests!"

But Nika's courage blazed hotter. "Father, you lied! You told me the British stole of our wealth, that only through my marriage could peace be restored. But I saw it with my own eyes—the English gold in our vault! They were not the thieves. We were! You used me as a pawn to cover your schemes, and you would have sold me off like cattle to fix your mistakes. I will not obey. I will not be part of this corruption!"

The king's fist slammed against the throne. "Rude, ill-mannered girl! Guards, seize her! Lock her in the north tower at once!"

But the queen rose to her feet, her face pale with fury. "No! I will not let you chain our daughter like a criminal. She has spoken truth, and you cannot silence her now."

"Silence, woman!" the king roared, his voice shaking the pillars. "This is no matter for you!"

The guards wavered, torn between orders. And in that moment of chaos, Nika acted. With a single motion, she hurled herself at the tall windows, teleporting, shattering glass in a spray of light. Then she was plunging into the sea below.

Cold water embraced her, and when she surfaced, she gasped with freedom. Dragging herself ashore, she sprinted toward the beach, her wet clothes clinging, her hair flying wild behind her.

There…waiting as if fate itself had arranged it, stood Alex, Ios, and Lucas. Their eyes widened as they saw her running towards them, soaked and breathless, but burning with resolve.

"The day has come," Nika cried. "Are you with me?"

A heavy silence hung in the air.

Ios swallowed hard. "But Nika... how can we sail away? We don't even have a ship."

Nika's lips curved into a daring smile. "Don't worry. The ship is ready. It's waiting for us at berth."

Alex's fists clenched with excitement. "Then let's not waste another second!"

Using her magical power, she teleported them to the ship. The ropes snapped loose, the wind caught, and the ship lurched forward.

Nika took the helm, her eyes fixed on the horizon. Behind her lay the palace, the kingdom, her father's tyranny. Ahead lay freedom. Adventure. Destiny.

And so, the White Ghost and her loyal crew sailed out over the new horizons…

Part II: The Beginning of a legend

Chapter 9: Freedom

Do you think this is the end of the story? No, it's only the beginning of new adventures. The beginning of a legend.

From the day she left her father's palace, years passed. Nika grew up. She was no longer the sheltered princess, hidden behind stone walls and governesses' lessons. She had become a pirate, but not like the ones she once despised as a child. No, she was different. She sailed the seas with her crew—her friends, her brothers, her chosen family.

No one knew their real names, no one knew where they came from. They were shadows on the waves, appearing and disappearing like spirits. All they ever left behind was a single mark scorched into wood, or painted onto sails, or carved into stone: N.K.

Nika Kassia.

The name struck fear into slavers, poachers, and warlords. But to the poor, the powerless, and the innocent—it was the name of hope. Pirates and sailors alike whispered another name when they spoke of her and her companions: "The White Ghost."

Nika had changed. The magic crystal she once received in a dream from the dolphin prince had awakened strange gifts within her. She could teleport across decks in the blink of an eye. She could vanish into thin air and reappear when least expected. She could speak and understand any living creature—birds, wolves, lions, snakes, even insects. With a cry, she could emit an ultrasonic wave that broke chains or scattered enemies into panic.

But her gifts grew beyond that. By helping magical beings across her travels, she was rewarded with fragments of their powers—water, fire, wind, and earth. Elemental sparks flowed within her veins. Nika had become more than human—she was a bridge between worlds.

Her ship was no less extraordinary. At first, it was a modest vessel, but through the years she and her crew rebuilt it plank by plank, guided by the compass and the whispers of the sea. It was strong, fast, and silent on the waves. They painted its sails white, and in the moonlight it looked like a phantom gliding across the ocean. No one ever saw them coming.

Alex, once the reckless boy who laughed at her dreams, had grown into her right hand—a skilled swordsman and strategist. Ios became the sharp-eyed scout, able to spot danger from miles away, his falcon emblem flying proudly on the mast. Lucas, strong and loyal, became the heart of the crew, a bear in strength but gentle with those they saved. Together, they were more than pirates. They were guardians of the seas.

Their missions became the stuff of songs and legends. In the port of Carthage, they freed children chained to galleys, breaking locks with Nika's ultrasonic voice and vanishing with the tide. In India, they fought poachers who hunted elephants and tigers, returning the animals to their forests. In the frozen North, they broke the chains of entire tribes enslaved by a cruel warlord. Every time they disappeared like mist, leaving only the carved mark of N.K.

And always, wherever Nika went, she was never alone. By her side swam the dolphin she once saved as a child. His name was Zack.

Zack was not only her companion but her protector, messenger, and guide. When storms rage, his clicks and whistles led the ship through the black waters. When enemies closed in, Zack rallied pods of dolphins, sometimes even whales, to crash against hostile vessels. To Nika, Zack was more than a friend. He was family.

So, the years passed, and the legend of the White Ghost grew. But legends have enemies, too. And Nika's greatest adventure—the one that would test not just her power, but her heart and her destiny—was only just about to begin…

Chapter 10: The Island of Aibuquerque

One day, after completing another dangerous mission, Nika returned to the harbor where she had left her ship— the Victoria—only to find empty waters. The dock was bare, the moorings cut, and the familiar white sails were nowhere in sight. Her heart sank.

Her crew. Her brothers. Gone.

She asked frantic questions to the locals, sailors, merchants, even children on the street. But no one knew anything. Or at least, no one was willing to talk. Each shrug and denial felt like a stone sinking deeper in her chest.

Exhausted, she walked to the edge of the beach, where waves lapped against the rocks. Raising her hand, she gave a long, piercing call—a sound beyond human ears. And in an instant, the sea broke with foam, and Zack swam to her side. His sleek gray body sparkled in the fading light.

Nika knelt and whispered everything, her voice trembling for the first time in years. "Zack... they're gone. Victoria is gone. I need you. Find them. Find out what happened."

The dolphin clicked in answer, pressing his head against her palm in promise, before disappearing again beneath the waves.

Staying on the island of Aibuquerque was too dangerous. Rumors of spies and mercenaries buzzed in every tavern.

Someone wanted her out of the way, and she wouldn't give them the chance. So, without hesitation, Nika boarded the first ship leaving the harbor. She didn't even ask where it was bound—anywhere was better than here. Right?

The vessel belonged to Captain Lorenzo, a stout man with a sharp eye. When Nika offered her services as a sailor, he raised a brow but agreed. Instead of ropes or sails, however, he sent her to the galley.

"You'll help the cook, Joseph. Start by peeling potatoes."

So down she went into the hold, where the air smelled of grease, salt, and damp wood.

"What are you cooking today?" Nika asked cheerfully.

Joseph, a short, grumbling man with arms like barrels, slammed a sack of potatoes in front of her.

"Stop talking. And. Peel."

"Sounds great, but don't you use spices?" she teased.

He glared at her, knife in hand. "What are you talking about?"

"Oh, I have an idea. Wait here."

Before Joseph could shout, Nika vanished in a blink.

"Another bastard on my head." Said Joseph.

She dove headfirst into the abyss of the sea, the cold water rushing around her like an embrace. Guided by instinct, she searched the reefs until she found it: shimmering green seaweed with a sweet, almost honey-like scent. She tore off a bundle, surfaced, and reboarded the ship without a sound. Moments later, she was back in the hold, dripping wet but smiling.

33

"I brought spices!"

Joseph nearly dropped his knife. "Where in Hades did you—?"

She handed him the seaweed.

"Add this to the potatoes. You'll thank me later."

Suspicion clouded his face. "Are you mad? You want to poison us?"

But curiosity got the better of him. He sniffed, tasted— and froze. His eyes went wide. Then he took another bite.

"It's... a miracle!"

That evening, the crew gathered for dinner as usual, but the moment they tasted Joseph's potatoes, silence fell. Then shouts erupted.

"What is this?!"

"More! Give me more!"

"By Poseidon, Joseph, you've outdone yourself!"

Captain Lorenzo himself took a bite and banged his fist on the table. "By the gods! I've never eaten like this at sea. Tell us, Joseph, what sorcery is this?"

The cook scratched his head, embarrassed. "It's not me. It's... seaweed." He pointed to Nika. "She disappeared, then came back with some strange seaweed. I didn't believe her, but..." He gestured to the empty bowls.

Every eye turned to Nika. She stood calmly, arms folded, then finally said:

"It's called Kiy. A gift from the sea. On long journeys, it can replace meat or fish. It restores strength, heals faster than bread or wine, and never spoils."

34

The crew murmured in awe.

"Kiy..." the captain repeated slowly. His sharp eyes studied Nika with new respect. "You're full of surprises, girl."

Chapter 11: The Tale of Atlantis

"And how did you find out about them?" Captain Lorenzo finally asked, narrowing his eyes at her.

"From a friend of mine, Taria—she lives in Atlantis."

The deck erupted in laughter.

"Did you say Atlantis?" Lorenzo scoffed, shaking his head. His men burst out laughing along with him, slapping their knees, wiping tears from their eyes, mocking her words as if they were the greatest joke ever told.

"Yes," Nika answered calmly, unfazed by their ridicule.

But she didn't stop. Instead, she stood tall and let her voice ring above their laughter, continuing her tale.

"It was one calm spring day, my crew and I rested on Bai-Bai Island, a warm beach where the waves whispered like silver. That's when a pirate ship passed, and I felt something... strange. Through ultrasound, I heard her cries. There was a prisoner in the hold, locked in a glass box filled with water.

Curious and uneasy, I swam to the ship. Slipping silently into the hold, I saw her—a creature like a woman, yet glowing with a bluish-pearl light. We stared at each other in silence, my heart pounding. At last, I whispered, 'You can trust me.'

She nodded and said only, 'Then act.'

I struck the glass, and when our hands touched, light covered us. In the blink of an eye, we stood together on the shores of Bai-Bai. She told me her name was Taria, princess of Atlantis. I tried to introduce myself, but she cut me short.

'I know who you are are,' she said. 'I will find you. Thank you.'

And then she vanished into the horizon like the tide."

The men had stopped laughing now, leaning closer.

"The next morning, while preparing my ship to sail, I saw her again. Taria. She motioned for me to follow her into the water. 'Trust me. Do not fear. Everything will be well.'

I hesitated only a moment, but then I did. If anything happened, I told myself, I would swim back. But Taria's body lit with that same pearl glow, and she swirled around me faster and faster, creating a vortex of bubbles. My breath caught, my vision blurred, and for a moment I lost consciousness.

When I awoke, I was breathing underwater.

Taria smiled. 'Come,' she said. 'I will show you my home.'

And so, she took me to Atlantis."

Nika's voice grew softer, almost reverent.

"The king himself greeted me warmly. He thanked me for saving his daughters, and as a gift, he granted me the power to command water. I thanked him in return and dared to ask to stay. Only a few days, I said. He agreed.

36

But days became weeks. My crew must have worried, so I sent a message in a bottle, trusting Zack to deliver it. My navigator Alex would understand.

I stayed for a month. In that time, Taria showed me wonders beyond imagination—how Atlanteans live in harmony, what gifts they wield, the technology they use, the beauty of their world.

Yet she warned me: 'We are strong only in water. Though we can breathe air, our magic fades beyond the sea.'"

Nika paused, her eyes distant. "That is how I know Atlantis is real."

The deck was silent. The men leaned forward, caught between awe and disbelief. Then Captain Lorenzo giggled, trying to mask his unease.

"I don't believe a single word. Not about Atlanteans, not about magic. You spin a good tale, girl, but that's all it is."

Nika sighed. "Alright."

She lifted her hand toward the waves. The sea stirred. A low rumble grew louder and louder until a towering wall of water rose high over the ship. Gasps filled the air. Then, with a snap of her wrist, the wave froze in place, suspended like living glass.

Lorenzo's jaw dropped. The crew stumbled back in terror, eyes wide as dinner plates.

"Well?" Nika asked with a laugh. "And how about now?"

She flicked her wrist again, and turning to Lorenzo, she said: "Oops!"

The wave collapsed—not in destruction, but as a playful splash that drenched the entire deck. Sailors coughed and cursed, shaking their soaked clothes.

Captain Lorenzo, pale as chalk, ran to his cabin and locked the door. His men followed, scattering like frightened children. In moments, the deck was deserted.

Alone, Nika stood on the soaked planks, staring out across the endless horizon.

Her heart was heavy. Even with power enough to terrify a whole ship, she felt a hollow ache inside. Where was Victoria? Where was her crew?

She clenched her fists, the sea breeze whipping through her hair. Whatever it took, she would find them.

This was only the beginning.

Chapter 12: The Captain's Secret

Going to the stern of the ship, Nika climbed onto the railing and without hesitation dove into the dark sea. The water embraced her like an old friend. She whistled ultrasonically, her call echoing far beneath the waves.

Minutes later, a silver silhouette broke through the deep. Zack swam swiftly to her, his eyes shining in the moonlight.

"Did you find out anything about my ship?" Nika asked, hope trembling in her voice.

"Yes," Zack replied. "Your team is staying in Syracuse."

"Syracuse?" Nika's brow furrowed. "What did they forget there?"

"I don't know," Zack admitted, his tone unusually heavy. "But I'm afraid... they don't want to see you."

"What?" Her heart clenched. "Ha! I don't believe it. It cannot be possible! My crew would never turn away from me."

Zack swam in uneasy circles. "I only bring what I know. Their silence worries me."

Nika crossed her arms, defiance in her voice. "Then I will see with my own eyes. Only then will I believe it."

The dolphin tilted his head. "Where is this ship going?"

"To Genoa, in Italy," Nika answered.

"That is good," Zack said. "From Genoa, you can find the merchant ships Sword and Stardust. They both sailed to Syracuse."

Relief spread across Nika's face. She leaned down, hugging Zack tightly. "What would I do without you? Thank you, Zack."

Zack whistled softly before disappearing into the dark waters.

She climbed back on board. The moonlight dripped from her wet clothes, forming small puddles on the deck. Just then, the captain's door creaked open. Lorenzo stepped out, his face pale, eyes still unsettled from what had happened earlier.

He scanned the deck, muttering. "Where is she...?"

Not found no one. Not in the hold, not near the ropes, not even by the helm.

Suddenly, a splash of water echoed behind him. Nika stood there, wringing water from her hair as if nothing was unusual.

"Can't sleep, captain?" she teased

Lorenzo. "Where have you been?"

"I talked with my dolphin," Nika answered simply, her voice calm, almost playful.

The captain's eyes narrowed. "Come to my cabin. Immediately."

Nika shrugged. "As you wish." She followed.

The cabin smelled of salt, old leather, and half-drunk rum. Maps lay scattered across the desk, along with an iron compass and a pistol. Lorenzo closed the door sharply and leaned against it, staring at her with a stern, almost trembling expression.

"Why did you call?" Nika asked, her arms crossed.

"I want to ask you something," he said slowly.

"Why?" she smirked.

His voice dropped low, almost a growl. "Are you a pirate... or a witch? Do you want to destroy us, witch?"

Nika raised an eyebrow. "I want to get to Syracuse."

"Syracuse..." He repeated the word as if it carried poison. "What are you trying to hide, girl?"

Nika smirked again, and that was the final spark. Rage boiled over. In one furious stride he lunged forward, his hand clamping around her throat. He pressed hard, his eyes wild.

"I should hang you from the yardarm!" he shouted, his spit hot with rum.

But suddenly, his hand grasped at nothing. Nika was gone. His eyes darted in panic. He spun around and nearly collapsed—she was standing behind him, calm, her arms folded.

The captain's knees buckled. He fell to the floor, shaking.

Nika crouched beside him, smiling softly. "I told you, captain. I have certain abilities. But listen carefully—neither you nor your men are in danger. I only need to get to Genoa."

Lorenzo gasped for air, still in shock. His forehead glistened with sweat.

Nika leaned casually against his desk. She grabbed a bottle of rum, uncorked it, and drank two deep gulps. "I'm the same as you," she said lightly. Handing him the bottle, she added, "Drink, captain. You'll feel better."

Lorenzo snatched it greedily and drank until the bottle was nearly drained. His cheeks reddened, his eyes heavy.

Half drunk, he chuckled. "Maybe you know... ancient languages, eh?" His words tangled together, thick with liquor.

"Yes, I know a couple," Nika replied with a sly grin. "Do you need a translator?"

The captain laughed, wobbling, and from under his desk he was dragged out a massive leather-bound book. Its cover was cracked with age, the clasps rusted bronze. He opened it on the first page, shoving it towards her.

"Cccc... ccc... can you translate this... ancient text?" he stammered, swaying.

Nika reached out and took the book. The moment her fingers touched the old leather, a shock ran through her veins. Her eyes widened.

In her mind, words flared like lightning: It can't be…

Her breath caught. She recognized the markings.

This is the book… "Nouveau."

She whispered aloud: "Yes... I know this language. This is the Mayan tongue. The bird language."

Her hands trembled as she turned the brittle pages. The symbols glowed faintly, as if the book itself breathed with power.

Nika knew then—this was no ordinary relic. This book carried secrets that could change everything.

Chapter 13: The Hidden Secret

"Translate these inscriptions," said the captain, his words heavy with rum.

Nika took a deep breath and began to read aloud:

"Behind the hills of the seven winds, behind the bushes of the seven hills, there was an evergreen turtle, with bluish little men dancing in a round circle. There you will find your first key..."

The words echoed in the cabin, old and strange, carrying a rhythm of forgotten times.

"What the heck are you talking about?" Lorenzo muttered, his face twisting. He slammed his fist on the table, the rum bottle topping over.

"Until you translate the whole book to the end and point out where these places are—you will not go anywhere!" he roared.

Nika's eyes are glinted. Perfect. He doesn't know what he holds in his hands. I can use this.

With a flick of her wrist, a thin vortex of air circled the book. The first page tore free, vanishing into an invisible cocoon she spun around it. Before Lorenzo's drunken eyes could even blink, Nika clutched the stolen page, whispered a word, and disappeared in a flash of blue light.

The next moment she was underwater, swimming fast, clutching the page tightly to her chest. She needed Taria. Only the Atlanteans could tell her the truth of this mystical book.

Behind her, Lorenzo staggered out of the cabin, screaming:

"You witch! Come back here!"

His voice echoed across the deck. Sailors rushed up, rubbing sleep from their eyes. Navigator Santiago grabbed the captain's arm. "Captain, what's wrong?"

Lorenzo's face twisted, his eyes bloodshot. "She stole it—she stole from me!" He snorted like a bull, shoving Santiago aside and stomping back into his cabin. The men exchanged confused glances.

Far below, in the clear waters of Atlantis, Taria was swimming with her friend Diana when she saw Nika rushing towards them.

"Nika!" Taria swam up, embracing her tightly.

"Taria, how long has it been since we last met," Nika breathed, relief washing over her.

"An eternity," Taria smiled. "How is your father?"

"He is fine. But this time, I came for something else." Nika showed the torn page.

Diana's pearl-blue eyes widened. "The language of birds..." she whispered.

Taria took the page carefully. Nika, speaking telepathically now, asked: "Is this what I think it is?"

"Yes," Taria replied gravely. "I think so. We must show it to my father."

The three of them swam quickly towards the shimmering domes of Atlantis.

In the great throne room, carved from coral and lined with glowing shells, the king of Atlantis sat in majesty, his crown glimmering like sunlight under the sea.

"Hello, Nika," he said warmly. "It is good to see you again."

"Father, we need your help," Taria said, holding out the page.

"Speak, my daughter."

Nika explained everything—the captain, the book, the translation. The king studied the page, turning it slowly in his hands. His face grew grave.

"I thought this book was only legend," he murmured. "The Nouveau. I believed the temple was destroyed. Yet here it is before me. Long ago, the Mayans visited the Temple of the Seven Seas. They stole forbidden knowledge from there... and with it, the book. No one was meant to carry it. The Temple is a forbidden place. No mortal should set foot inside."

"The Temple still exists?" Nika asked, her heart pounding.

The king nodded solemnly. "It exists. And people are drawn to it for one reason only—gold. Endless gold."

"Gold..." Nika clenched her fists. "Then that is why the pirates want it."

"They are sailing to Genoa," Nika continued. "But for what purpose?"

"They want a translator," the king said darkly. "Someone who can read the Mayan tongue. That is their only chance."

"They won't succeed," Taria interrupted. "Even with the book, they will never find Shan Island. It is hidden, secured by the sea itself."

Nika raised her chin. "Then I must stop them. I will steal the book and hide it forever—from pirates, from kings, from all of humankind."

The king studied her carefully. Finally, he nodded. "I believe in you. You will succeed. And remember— Atlantis will be here when you need us."

That night, Nika and Taria swam back to the surface. The pirate ship was already docked at Genoa. Lanterns burned on the port, sailors shouting as cargo was carried.

"We must find the captain quickly," Nika whispered.

Meanwhile, in a dark tavern by the docks, Captain Lorenzo leaned over a wooden table, the book lying open before him. Across from him sat a man with sharp eyes and long, ink-stained fingers—Ikiz, the translator.

"Hello, captain. Good to see you," Ikiz said slyly.

"Hello, Ikiz. I have business with you."

"I understand. Please, sit." His voice was oily, cunning.

Lorenzo slide the book across. "Can you translate this?"

Ikiz leafed through the pages slowly, muttering strange sounds, his eyes narrowing with every line. Finally, he looked up.

"And what will I get for it?" he asked.

"Whatever you want. Name your price."

Ikiz smirked, tapping the torn edge. "Rest in peace, captain—you won't fool me. The first page is missing."

"I know!" Lorenzo bellowed. His face turned red. "Some devil stole it from me. Will you still translate?"

Ikiz leaned back in his chair, rubbing his chin, his eyes gleaming with greed. "Hmm... I need to think. Think carefully..."

"Think fast, Ikiz!" Lorenzo slammed his fist on the table.

At that moment, a shadow passed outside the tavern window. Nika was there, watching, her hand tightening around the page she had saved.

They won't get this book, she thought. Not while I'm alive.

Chapter 14: Clash at Sea

"Ikiz!"

With one leap, Captain Lorenzo lunged across the tavern, seizing Ikiz by the chest of his tunic and slamming him hard against the shelf of dusty books.

"Don't play games with me!" Lorenzo growled, his breath hot with rum. "I will bury you under the ground if I must. Now listen carefully—on the first page, the writing spoke of an evergreen turtle... and the Atlanteans. Do not deny it."

Ikiz gasped for air, clawing at Lorenzo's wrist. "Let me go, captain. I only need to fetch one book from this shelf... it is for business. For business, I wear."

Suspicious, Lorenzo narrowed his eyes but loosened his grip. Ikiz staggered to the shelf, grabbed a heavy volume, and opened it on a yellowed page. There, in faded ink, was an illustration: bluish figures—Atlanteans—dancing in a circle around a turtle-shaped island.

"This," Ikiz said with a sly smile, "is the island of Atlantes. It lies in the Devil's Place. A cursed region. No one knows exactly where."

"Don't lie to me, Ikiz, or I'll..." Lorenzo's hand snapped to the man's throat again.

"It's true! I swear it on my life," Ikiz wheezed.

"You will come with me," Lorenzo snarled, shoving him forward, "and you will show me this island."

They stormed towards the port, Lorenzo dragging Ikiz by the collar like a dog on a chain. But before they could reach the docks, a figure stepped out of the shadows.

"You?!" Nika's voice cut the night.

Lorenzo froze, then smirked darkly. "You? Back already, brat? Did you decide to return my paper?"

"Ha, never ever," Nika hissed, drawing her saber with a sharp ring of steel. "I came to kill you and take your book."

"Daring... but foolish." Lorenzo bared his teeth and pulled his own blade, the metal glinting in the moonlight.

"What a beautiful couple," Ikiz muttered with a grin.

"Shut up," Nika snapped. She lunged, blades clashing. Sparks flew as steel met steel. Her strikes were quick, fluid, each one pressing Lorenzo back. Yet his strength was brutal, every blow rattling her arms.

"You are making a big mistake," Nika warned between strikes.

"Who are you to teach me?" Lorenzo sneered, swinging harder.

Suddenly Nika stopped, lowering her blade. "I'm not here to waste time fighting you, another pirate skank. Hand me the book, and we leave it at that."

Lorenzo's eyes are narrowed. He glanced at Ikiz. "Do you know where this island lies?"

"No," Ikiz said quickly, sweat beading on his brow.

Lorenzo turned back. "Then tell me, witch—do you know?"

Nika's voice was calm, cold: "Even if I did, I would never tell you."

At that moment, a shadow moved behind her. Nika spun—and her blood froze. Navigator Santiago had Taria in his grip, the edge of his saber pressed to her throat.

"Taria, no!" Nika cried.

"Think carefully, witch," Lorenzo taunted. "Either your blue friend dies... or you surrender. Your choice."

Nika's heart pounded. Her hand clenched around her saber. But seeing Taria's frightened eyes, she slowly lowered her weapon. "I'll come with you," she said through gritted teeth.

"Good girl." Lorenzo smirked.

They dragged her aboard the pirate ship. As they climbed the deck, Nika caught Taria's gaze and gave a quick blink. A secret signal. In the next instant, she summoned her Atlantean strength and unleashed a towering wave across the deck. Water thundered over the ship, knocking men off their feet. Amid the chaos, Nika snatched the book from Lorenzo's belt and pulled Taria toward the railing.

They almost made it. Nika's foot was already on the edge when Lorenzo lunged like a beast, his dagger flashing. The blade slashed Taria's leg, and she crumpled with a cry.

"Taria!" Nika turned, fury blazing, fire crackling in her hands. She raised her magic to burn the captain alive— but froze at the sight of her wounded friend. She couldn't risk it.

"Hide them both in the hold!" Lorenzo roared. "Keep a close eye on them!"

In the darkness of the hold, Nika tore strips of cloth to bandage Taria's bleeding leg.

"You need water," Nika whispered. "Once you touch it, your wound will heal. I swear, we'll get out of here soon."

49

Taria feeling pain, forced a smile. "Don't worry about me. Worry about us. Where is your crew?"

"I don't know," Nika admitted, her voice breaking. She told Taria everything—about the missing ship, the vanished crew, Zack's warnings.

When she finished, Taria laid a hand on hers. "Then maybe... maybe we don't need them right now. We can find this temple ourselves. We can discover its secrets before anyone else. Isn't this what you dreamed of once?"

"Yes," Nika whispered, staring at the flickering lantern. "I did. But I gave up on that dream."

"The book exists. The temple too," Taria pressed. "Then let us be the ones to find it. Together."

Nika's heart pounded with both fear and excitement. She didn't answer—she couldn't. Not yet.

Suddenly, a shout from the deck:

"Straight ahead—a British frigate!"

The crew rushed to the rails. Out of the fog loomed a massive warship, its sails white as bone. Cannons glinted in the dawn light. The two ships halted side by side, and a boarding plank slammed down.

Prince Charles himself strode across, flanked by armed soldiers.

"What are you carrying, pirates?" Charles demanded, his voice sharp.

"Nothing," Lorenzo spat back.

"Open the hold," Charles ordered.

The soldiers stormed below and found Nika crouched beside wounded Taria.

"Pick them up," Charles commanded, fury in his eyes.

"You will not take them!" Lorenzo roared, drawing his blade.

And with that, the deck erupted into chaos—pirates and soldiers clashing steel against steel, the sea itself trembling under the fury of battle.

Part III: The Water and Island

Chapter 15: The White Ghost Betrayed

The clash of steel rank across the deck. The British frigate had cast its shadow over Lorenzo's ship, and now soldiers in red coats poured across the planks, sabers flashing, pistols firing. The pirates answered with roars and muskets, and the whole sea seemed to tremble under their fury.

Nika held Taria close, shielding her from flying splinters as cannons roared. Smoke and salt filled the air. The chaos gave her one thought: This is the chance.

Lorenzo bellowed like a mad bull, cutting down soldier after soldier. Charles, standing tall amidst his men, shouted orders that were carried across the din. "Forward! Drive them back! For the Crown!"

Nika gritted her teeth, torn between helping the British or letting the pirates be destroyed. But when she saw

Santiago charging towards her and Taria, blade raised, her decision was made.

Raising her hand, she summoned the sea. A column of water surged up from nowhere and crashed onto the deck, sweeping pirates and soldiers alike off their feet. The ship groaned under the weight of the water, and silence fell for a brief moment.

Everyone froze.

Taria's voice, clear as a bell, rang out above the stunned silence:

"Prince Charles—we sail with you."

Gasps followed. And before Lorenzo or his men could recover, Nika and Taria limped toward Charles, crossing the blood-stained deck. Charles, realizing what was happening, motioned his soldiers back. "Protect them!" he barked.

Together, they crossed to the British frigate. The gangplank was pulled away, and the ships drifted apart. The pirates howled in fury, but Nika didn't look back.

On the frigate's deck, Charles studied her face. His expression softened, his voice almost trembling:

"You... you remind me of someone. Have we met before?"

Nika gave a sly laugh, dipped into a mocking curtsey, and said:

"Nika Kassia, at your service. We were supposed to marry, remember?"

Charles staggered back as if struck. "Nika... is it truly you?"

She nodded.

Joy flooded his face. He rushed forward, seizing her shoulders. "By God! I don't believe my eyes! You're alive! How—where have you been? Tell me everything, quickly!"

"I'll tell you in time," Nika said firmly. "For now—where are you sailing?"

"To Syracuse. To meet the king... your father."

Nika's eyes are hardened. "Just what I needed."

Before Nika could say more, she turned to Taria. They had already agreed—Taria would return to the sea to heal her wounded leg. With a nod, the princess slipped into the water, her bluish glow vanishing beneath the waves.

The frigate sailed swiftly, and soon the towers of Syracuse rose from the horizon.

The moment the ship docked, Nika leapt from the deck, her boots pounding the planks as she ran to the harbor where Victoria, her ship, had once been. She found it quickly—yet what she saw froze her blood.

The ship was empty. Completely stripped. No crew. No weapons. No personal belongings. Nothing. It was as though it had never been theirs.

Her heart sank. Where are they?

She remembered Charles's words—his meeting with the king. A flicker of intuition told her, her team would be there. Without hesitation, she teleported, appearing silently inside the palace. Landing light as a shadow on the marble floor, she pressed herself against a column, invisible, and listened.

Inside the grand chamber, Charles stood before the king.

"Your Majesty, I want to discuss the details of our agreement," Charles said.

"I am listening," the king replied gravely.

"Do not forget, we need not only strong soldiers—but also men who know the ancient languages."

The king raised his hand. Servants brought in a group of young men. Nika's heart stopped. Alex. Ios. Lucas. Her brothers-in-arms.

"Charles," Alex said boldly, "we are ready for anything. We are tired of serving a captain who failed us."

"Very good," Charles nodded. "And you are not afraid of the White Ghost?"

Ios smirked. "No. Because the White Ghost is no longer with us."

Lucas added coldly, "The White Ghost is eliminated."

Nika's breath caught. Her chest tightened as if pierced.

And then Ios spoke the words that shattered her:

"The White Ghost is the most despicable, unbearable creature alive. Good riddance."

The words stabbed deeper than any blade. Tears blurred her vision, but her fury burned hotter. She could not stay hidden any longer.

With a crack of displaced air, she teleported before them, saber drawn. In one swift motion she pressed the blade against Ios's throat. Gasps erupted through the hall.

"Where did you come from?" Charles demanded, stunned.

Nika's voice shook with rage and sorrow:

"You betrayed me—for gold. You are pitiful, worthless creatures who do not deserve to live in this world."

Alex stepped forward, eyes blazing. "You're the one in the way, Nika! You've always been selfish—spoiled— never letting us prove ourselves. You are the most arrogant and capricious girl alive!"

Her tears fell freely now. She raised her saber high, then lowered it slowly. Her voice rank like thunder across the chamber:

"Then hear me well. I will find the Temple of the Seven Seas. And I will claim everything within it—alone. Because I am the White Ghost!"

With that, she vanished in a flash of light, teleporting to the shore. Her heart is still broken, she ran to the water, searching for Taria—to tell her everything.

Chapter 16: The Pact of the Ghost

"I cannot believe my ears, she's the White Ghost, she has changed so much from our wedding." Charles asked the crew. "It there a way to stop her?"

"We, captain, will help you stop her, but at the beginning you need to know that Nika has changed a lot and became a witch who has no forgiveness, and who must burn in hell. She has incredible strength and many different abilities. However, every time she uses her power, she gets tired very quickly and becomes weak from it." Alex replied.

"Let's not waste time." Charles said.

Meanwhile, Nika met with Taria and told her about everything that happened.

Comforting Nika, Taria said:

"They don't understand what they're doing. They are acting like kids." Calmly said Taria hugging Nika.

"It's my fault, most likely," Nika took a deep breath. "When I was very young, I was given many abilities, and I used them trying to do everything myself. Almost on every task I went myself, without involving the team. I didn't do it for selfish reasons as it may have seemed to the team. I did it because…because I was afraid to put them in danger, I really valued each of them, and if something happened to them, I wouldn't…I wouldn't forgive myself for this. But from this side, unfortunately, it seemed as if I wanted to take all the glory for myself. I feel very hurt and offended, but I do not blame them."

Taria hugged Nika in a friendly way and said:

"Forget them. We will find the book and the temple, and you will restore friendship and prove to your team that they where wrong."

"Let's sail to Lorenzo." answered Nika and they swam to the ship.

Soon the girls climbed onto the deck.

Nika shouted:

"Captain, where the heck are you?"

"Who is there screaming there on the deck!" leaving his cabin, the captain asked:

"It's you? What are you doing here?"

"Captain, I want to offer you a deal."

"I don't deal with witches."

"If I translate the whole book and show where is every key to the temple are, then will we agree?!"

"You're all lying."

"No, I came to negotiate with you. Most of gold is your captain. 90% yours and plus I protect you from all problems along your way."

"You can't protect me from the White Ghost." said the captain.

"I am the White Ghost, so 90% and my help. Agree?

The captain laughed, and through laughter said:

"Prove it."

Nika in the blink of an eye moved to the cabin captain, took the book on the table, leaving her initials. The captain did not have time to blink, as Nika again was already on deck with a book in her hands.

"Here is your book," Nika said, "Now go to cabin and look at your table."

The captain's face changed, he went like a bullet to cabin and was dumbfounded when he saw on the table the initials of the White Ghost.

Nika's words still echoed in the captain's ears as he stared at the table with the initials N.K. scratched deep into the oak. His hand trembled. Never before had he seen anyone move with such swiftness, such unexplainable strength.

"So, do you agree?" Nika's voice whispered right behind his ear, cold as steel.

Lorenzo shuddered. Sweat rolled down his forehead, his lips stammered.

"I...I...I...agree."

"Good," Nika said briskly. "Then let's begin. No time to waste."

She set the book down, opened the torn first page that she had hidden before, and tapped it with her finger. "First step is clear. We must find the Evergreen Turtle, with the Atlanteans."

Lorenzo squinted. "Where is this turtle?"

Before Nika could answer, a ripple of blue light filled the cabin. Taria stepped out from the shadows, her presence glowing faintly like the sea at night.

"This is the island of Shan," Taria said calmly. "The island of the Atlanteans. It lies in the heart of the Devil's Triangle, hidden from mortal eyes. We have guarded it for centuries."

The captain swallowed hard. "Devil's Triangle...so it is true."

"Yes," Nika replied with a smirk. "And you're sailing us straight into it."

Chapter 17: Voyage Into the Triangle

For weeks, the ship carved across the ocean. At first, the voyage seemed ordinary—calm winds, clear skies, playful gulls wheeling above. Yet with each passing day, the tension grew heavier among the crew.

Some whispered that the woman on board was cursed. Others muttered she was no woman at all but some spirit of the deep, come to drag them all beneath the waves. Some called her a witch, others a demon. Sailors spat when she passed. But none dared touch her, for they had seen the wave she summoned, the speed with which she vanished and reappeared, the strange calm in her eyes when the sea raged. They feared her more than the storms themselves.

Nika paid them no mind. She spent her hours on deck, staring into the endless horizon, her hand always brushing the cover of the book as though it anchored her. At night, she trained—vanishing and reappearing, testing the limits of her strength. Each time she used her powers, her body weakened, sweat dripping, breath ragged. But she pressed on, as though preparing for a trial greater than anyone could imagine.

Meanwhile, Taria recovered slowly, spending her nights in barrels filled with seawater, her pearl-blue glow shimmering faintly in the dark. Some sailors crossed themselves when they saw it, others bowed their heads. None dared speak to her, but many watched from the shadows, caught between awe and terror.

Then, one stormy evening, the sea turned black. Not dark with night, but black as ink, as if the ocean itself had become a living void. Waves crashed over the deck, tearing ropes loose, snapping masts like twigs. The air reeked of salt and lightning.

"The Triangle!" one sailor screamed above the roar. "We've reached the cursed waters!"

The storm howled like demons set loose. Lightning split the sky into jagged shards. The ship groaned, timbers bending, threatening to tear apart. Sailors clung to the rigging, some praying to saints, others cursing the day they'd signed on. One dropped to his knees, weeping, whispering names of children he would never see again.

Then Nika walked to the bow, rain hammering her face, hair whipping wild like a banner of war. She raised both hands.

The sea answered.

A wall of water rose, towering over the ship like a living mountain, blotting out the stars. The crew cried out, certain their doom had come. Some buried their faces, others drew knives pointlessly, as if steel could wound the sea.

But Nika's voice cut through the storm—clear, sharp, unyielding:

"Obey me!"

The wall bent, parted, and split the waves in two. A channel of calm opened, a glassy path stretching into the heart of the maelstrom. The ship slid into it, cradled by stillness while chaos raged on every side.

The crew fell silent. No one prayed now. No one cursed. They only stared.

From that moment, whispers changed. No longer did they call her witch alone. Now, trembling, they called her something else—

the White Ghost.

Chapter 18: Mutiny and Fire

But fear quickly turned to envy.

One night, while the captain slept and Taria meditated in her water barrel, a group of sailors cornered Nika near the mainmast.

"You've bewitched us long enough," snarled their leader. "This is our ship, not yours!"

He raised his blade.

Nika didn't flinch. In one motion, she vanished—and appeared behind him. She whispered into his ear: "You should not have done that."

Before he could turn, she pressed two fingers to his chest and released a spark of fire. His shirt ignited, flames leaping high. The others staggered back in horror as the man screamed and dove into the sea.

Nika's eyes glowed in the darkness. "Anyone else?"

No one answered. The mutiny died before it had begun.

Still, her strength drained. She sank to her knees, gasping, sweat pouring down her face. The men saw her weakness—and learned the truth of Alex's words: each power cost her dearly.

Chapter 19: Shadows of Shan

At last, after weeks of storms and silence, the waters grew calm. The sky burned crimson at dawn, and ahead of them shimmered something impossible—an island half-hidden in mist, its sands glowing faintly blue, as if made of crystal.

"Lead us, Taria," said Nika, stepping out from the captain's cabin, her eyes fixed on the strange horizon.

"Spirits of water, sea creatures, show the way to our native home, to our haven..." Taria began to sing, walking slowly in circles around the ship's deck. Her voice was soft yet powerful, like the sea itself.

The sailors exchanged uneasy glances.

"Why is she singing?" asked Lorenzo, narrowing his eyes.

"She summons the water spirits to open way to Shan Island," Nika answered calmly.

As if to prove her words, a streak of light appeared upon the water, glowing silver-white and stretching towards the distant mist. It shimmered like a path carved through the ocean.

"Captain, follow the line."

"Understood. Hey, you lazy rats, full sails! Stay the course along that glow!" Lorenzo barked.

The ship shifted, catching the wind, moving steadily along the strange, ethereal lane. Nika approached Taria.

"At this speed, we'll sail two weeks or more. And given that Charles knows about our plans, he can catch up. We need to hurry. Hold on, Taria—there will be a strong wind now."

Nika closed her eyes, raised her hands, and began to summon air.

In an instant, the sails swelled, and the ship surged forward with unnatural force. The crew cried out as they tumbled across the deck, clutching ropes, barrels, and each other. Nika ran to the helm, seized it, and steered the ship through the speeding waves. For four long hours the ship tore across the sea like a phantom, but Nika's face grew pale, her lips trembling.

…Wohoo, why you need diesel to fuel a boat, if you can call White Ghost to summon a wind…But any way…

At last, her strength failed—her body gave in—and she collapsed unconscious onto the deck.

Taria screamed and ran to her. "Nika!"

Lorenzo rushed forward, lifted her into his arms, and carried her below.

The crew gathered around Taria. "What's wrong with her? Did the witch finally kill herself with her spells?" one of the sailors whispered nervously.

Taria's eyes flashed. "If a mortal receives magic from us—magical creatures—they can use it only for a limited time. Otherwise, the magic will drain all their strength. Magic is energy, and energy burns quickly. It must be restored. We Atlanteans are immortal, and it is easier for us. But humans..."

"Does that mean we are weak?" asked one sailor.

"Yes. That is why you live less than we do."

"How old are you then?" sneered Santigo, crossing his arms.

"I am one hundred and sixty-nine. In a month, I'll be one hundred and seventy," Taria answered.

The deck roared with laughter. "A grandma of the sea! Don't tell us stories, girl!"

But Taria only smiled faintly, her eyes far older than they wanted to believe.

It took Nika two days to recover. When she finally stepped onto the deck, the sun was high, and the sea glittered like liquid silver. But her joy of recovery quickly shattered when she caught sight of a shadow on the horizon.

A frigate. And not just any frigate.

The British colors snapped in the wind.

"What is he doing here?" Taria gasped.

"It cannot be... How did they catch us?" Nika ran to the captain. "Lorenzo! We need to run away from the British frigate. He wants the book!"

She pointed at the looming sails growing closer.

"Then what are you waiting for? Act!" Lorenzo barked.

"Everyone, to the hold!" Nika shouted. "Taria—into the water! Push the ship with waves, and I will try to create a vortex of air!"

The sea boiled with Taria's power as waves rose behind them like hands, shoving the ship forward. Nika spread her arms, her hair whipping wildly, summoning a whirling tunnel of wind that caught their sails and yanked them across the waves.

The frigate faltered, falling behind.

"They're turning away!" shouted a sailor.

But across the sea, on the British ship, Charles lowered his spyglass, his brow folded up.

"She sails in the opposite direction," he muttered.

Lucas leaned close. "According to my observations, Nika is predictable. She wants to deceive us, but I think she's steering away only to loop back. If we sail to Iota first, we can cut her path."

"Iota?" Charles asked.

"It's a pirate city," Ios explained.

Alex stepped forward, eyes glamming. "I have a plan to catch her, captain. But yes—we'll have to go to Iota."

"I'm listening," Charles said coldly.

Meanwhile, Zack had swum alongside Lorenzo's ship, calling out with his dolphin-cry. Taria dove in at once.

"Zack, what's wrong?"

"Where is Nika? I must speak with her."

"She's busy fighting the wind," Taria answered. "Tell me instead."

"Her team is with Prince Charles," Zack said gravely.

Taria's eyes softened. "We already knew... She heard them betrayal with her own ears. They made their pact with him."

Zack circled restlessly. "Then the legends must be true. The book is found. The temple exists."

"Yes," Taria whispered. "But do you know? Only the chosen one can pass the main test of the Temple of the Seven Seas…"

The words hung heavy over the water, as though the sea itself was listening.

Chapter 20: The Whale's Secret

…Interesting, should I get a popcorn or continue this story…

"Yes, of course I know," Zack said in a low voice, "and I also know that the one who passes the test will receive a reward from the gods and will fulfill his most conspicuous desire. Wish for anything."

"That is why I want to help Nika," Taria insisted.

"I'm sorry, I can't go to the temple with you."

"Why won't you tell her everything? Are you going to hide all your life? It's your sister—why don't you tell her?"

"You know very well why."

"Soooo...she can remove the spell from you in the Temple—"

"Taria!" Zack interrupted firmly. "I have lived in this form all my life, and I know I can't become a human ever again. Let her live her own life." And with one powerful flip of his tail, Zack swam into the darkness of the sea.

Taria sighed, whispering to herself:

"How will she ever guess you're her brother...? And how will she help you if you keep acting foolish again?"

That evening, the sea turned black. Clouds strangled the stars, and thunder rolled as though the gods themselves were quarreling. The ship heaved from side to side, boards creaking.

"I'm afraid... this is a Hylos wave," whispered Taria, staring into the storm. "It can sink a ship."

"Then we must leave—now!" Nika said. She dashed across the deck, rain soaking her hair, and burst into Lorenzo's cabin.

"Captain! We have to abandon ship. Now!"

Lorenzo scoffed, his eyes flashing stubbornly. "Are you a fool? I will not leave my ship."

Nika clenched her jaw. No time for arguing. She snatched the book of the Seven Seas from his desk, pressed it against her chest, and whistled ultrasonically, her voice piercing the thunder.

"Captain," she said one last time, "if we don't leave now, we all go to the bottom together."

The ship is cracked. The deck tore apart as water poured in. Sailors screamed. In seconds, the proud vessel was no longer a ship, but splinters sinking into the abyss.

And then—it came.

A giant shadow surged up from beneath, vaster than the ship itself. A mouth opened, cavernous and shimmering with water. With one sweep, the massive blue whale swallowed the rushing sea—sailors and wreckage along with it.

The world went dark.

Inside the belly of the beast, the crew struggled for breath. The walls were slick with saltwater, glowing faintly as if the whale itself carried the light of the deep.

Taria's body shimmered with her Atlantean glow, casting blue halos across the stunned men.

"This... this is how it feels to be inside a whale," muttered Lorenzo, gawking in disbelief.

Nika, standing tall despite the chaos, placed her hand against the pulsing wall. "This is a blue whale. Larger than ordinary whales, and more aggressive to strangers than most. But kind to those it accepts. He's my puppy. I called him, and he came."

"Puppy? Called?" Lorenzo scowled. "I told you, you are a witch!"

"Instead of thanking me, you insult me," Nika shot back, crossing her arms. "How rude."

"How much longer must we… swim inside this monster?" Lorenzo grown.

"About a day, maybe two. We're close to Shan already. But it is guarded by Taria's brother, Hylos, and his army. It's they who raise this storm, weaving fog so that no mortal can approach."

"I don't care about storms," Lorenzo snapped. "But how in God's name did you tame such a beast?"

Nika's eyes softened, her voice dropping to a story-teller's hush.

"I'll tell you. It all started one summer, sailing toward the Isle of Skye, off the coast of Scotland. We stumbled upon a band of pirates who had captured a young blue whale. He was enormous already, but still a calf, his cries shaking the sea. They had chained him with iron hooks, driving spears into his sides, laughing at his suffering.

Something inside me snapped. I couldn't stand it."

She paused, her face darkening at the memory.

"They wanted to kill him, and then sell him on the black market for a mountain of gold," Nika continued, her voice firm yet quiet. "Hearing the groans of Bubbles, I teleported to the island and killed the pirates, freeing the blue whale. I wanted to send him into the ocean, but he had huge wounds and cuts from harpoons, and obviously he could not swim. At that time, I decided to stay on the island for a while and take care of him."

The men of Lorenzo's crew leaned in, wide-eyed, some crossing themselves, some whispering about witches and miracles.

"From Taria I knew that ointment from the medicinal algae Ubiu heals any wounds quickly. I prepared the ointment and smeared it on his wounds, and at night I fed him a soup of shells and mussels. Two weeks passed, and he eventually recovered. Before saying goodbye, he told me that if I ever needed help, he would come to my aid."

The captain frowned but his voice carried doubt more than mockery:

"I can believe that you cured the whale, and I can even believe you killed pirates with magic. But how in Neptune's name did you understand whale-talk?"

Nika smiled faintly. "One of my powers, given to me in gratitude for my help, is the ability to understand any living creature."

"And how did you get this ability?" Lorenzo pressed, almost childlike with curiosity.

Nika looked to the horizon. "That's another story. When I was a child, the dolphin Zack—yes, the same one who follows me to this day—gave me my first gift of power, in exchange for saving his life. That is how I first spoke the language of the sea."

The captain shook his head slowly. "You are no ordinary girl."

69

The voyage inside the belly of Bubbles lasted another day and night. At last, the whale broke the surface, letting out a mighty squeal that echoed like a horn across the endless fog. He opened his cavernous mouth wide, letting the men and women spill onto a stretch of glowing sand.

The crew staggered forward, coughing, covered in salt and seaweed.

But there was no time to rest.

From the mist, Atlanteans appeared. Dozens of them. They moved like shadows, swift and silent, their tridents glimmering with blue light. Their eyes burned with the fury of guardians.

The sailors froze, hands twitching near sabers, but they knew in their bones these were no enemies they could match.

Then Nika and Taria ran forward, speaking in the flowing, melodic tongue of the Atlanteans. The air itself seemed to hum with their words. They begged, reasoned, proclaimed—until the soldiers lowered their tridents, hesitating.

From behind them stepped a tall figure in shining coral armor, his hair streaming like silver across his shoulders. His eyes were hard as obsidian.

"Hylos," Taria whispered, her lips trembling.

The Prince of Atlantis strode forward, gaze locking on his sister. His voice thundered like waves against cliffs.

"Sister... what are you doing here—with her?" He pointed at Nika as if naming a curse.

Taria's face softened into a smile, her eyes glistening. "I am glad to see you too, brother. I owe her my life." She leaned closer, whispering words only he could hear.

But Hylos's face remained stone. "I will not let you risk your life for this... human." His contempt towards Nika was plain, his voice a blade.

"First, she saved me, and I am indebted," Taria said firmly. "Second, can you imagine—? The Temple truly exists! With her help, we may discover secrets beyond even Atlantis."

Hylos's tighten jawed. "I don't want you near that cursed place. What will I tell our father if you vanish forever?"

Taria reached out, clasping his arm. "Brother, trust me. I will return safe. We need this island for only a short while. Please—dismiss your army."

Hylos stared into her eyes, then exhaled heavily, defeated. "One hour. No more."

He raised his hand, and the Atlantean guards melted back into the mist, leaving only the whisper of waves.

Meanwhile, Lorenzo had his eyes fixed on Nika. The moment the soldiers were gone, he pressed forward, his hand resting on his saber.

"Now...White Ghost. Where is the key to the Temple?"

Nika turned slowly, her gaze cold but steady.

"You are standing on it."

The captain's face twisted. "What trick are you playing at now?"

Nika knelt, pressing her palm to the glowing sands. The beach shimmered with light, as if the entire island itself was alive. A faint hum rose from beneath, like a sleeping heart waiting to wake.

She looked up, her eyes blazing.

"The first key is not an object. It is a place. Shan itself."

Chapter 21: The First Key

"The book says that, after passing the water world, you will need to find the first key located on the abdomen of the turtle," Nika read aloud.

"What?" Lorenzo barked, frowning.

"Are we going to have to search the whole island?" muttered Santigo.

"The crystal could be the key," Taria suggested softly, her eyes narrowing towards the sea.

Nika thought for a moment. "No. The belly of the turtle... it must be under the water. Maybe it's a cave?"

Taria's face lit up as memory stirred. "When I was little, I remember... beneath the waves there was a strange stone wall. Maybe that was the belly of the turtle."

"Then what are we wasting time for? Into the water!" the captain ordered.

"Hold on—how do you imagine going under there? You can't breathe in water!" Nika snapped.

"I agree. It's pointless to drag the whole crew. Hey, you land rats, stay on the island! Santigo—you're with me."

Without another word, Lorenzo plunged into the sea. Santigo cursed under his breath but followed.

Nika rolled her eyes and shook her head. "Idiots. Taria, give them the ability to breathe underwater, or they'll choke on salt before finding anything."

Taria raised her hands, whispering a spell, and a faint glow passed over the men. Then, with Nika and Taria beside them, all four swam down into the depths.

The water grew darker, colder, until at last a colossal wall appeared, its stones smooth as if carved by gods themselves.

"Taria... is that the cave you spoke of?" Nika whispered through the water.

Yes. But it looks sealed." Taria swam closer, her eyes scanning the surface until she found a faint ledge, etched with runes long eroded. She touched it.

The ocean trembled. The wall shuddered, groaning as if it were alive, then slowly sank into the earth. The abyss yawned open before them.

They swam inside.

The passage was narrow, black as midnight, until suddenly they broke through the surface into an air-filled chamber. Light blinded them—an unnatural, dazzling glow that poured from a single object suspended high in the cavern's heart.

It was a crystal, bright blue, hanging weightless in the air, humming with power.

"Blow me down!" Lorenzo gasped. "Is this the first key?"

"Probably," Nika said, her voice steady but her heart racing. "But how do we reach it? It's too high."

"Since it is a crystal of water, it must answer to water's magic," Taria said. She spread her arms, weaving an unseen symphony. The pool below them rose, twisting upward like a serpent toward the levitating crystal. The glow flickered—but the stone refused to move.

Exhaustion took her. She fell to her knees.

"Does... does the book say anything about how to take it?" she gasped.

Nika frowned, scanning the old text. "Nothing. But let me try."

She stepped forward, summoning her power. Wind swirled around the chamber, echoing like a storm. She reached upward—but the crystal only pulsed brighter, rejecting her.

"What a bloody damn crystal!" Lorenzo roared.

"No... it is sealed," Taria whispered. "The seal of eternity, the most powerful magic among the Atlanteans and the most ancient. It hasn't been used for over 3000 years." Taria replied.

"Taria, with a song of sirens, we can take it down. I will start to sing, and you will pick up." Nika suggested.

She began softly, her voice a gentle hum that ripped through the air. Then louder, rising, a siren's call filling the cavern. Taria joined her, her Atlantean tones weaving with Nika's melody. The chamber vibrated, the water churned, and the crystal pulsed—glowing brighter, brighter—until, with a great shudder, it descended.

"The crystal, it glows!" Santigo shouted.

"Hurry and catch it!" bellowed Lorenzo.

Nika leapt, her fingers closing around the stone. A surge of energy coursed through her body, blue light wrapping her in a radiant aura.

"Oh, mighty power of the ancestors... You are glowing!" Taria cried, awe-struck.

But then the cavern roared. The walls shook, rocks splintering from the ceiling.

"Out! Now!" Lorenzo shouted.

They dove back into the water, racing down the corridor as the cave collapsed around them. Stones crashed, currents surged, the sea itself seemed to want to bury them. But they burst from the entrance just in time, shooting upward toward the surface.

They staggered onto the shore of Shan, gasping for breath, drenched and trembling.

Nika still clutched the crystal, its glow faint but steady.

"Now we are one step closer then, this British arrogant snob is. Ha, ha." Said Santigo.

But before relief could settle, a slow clap broke the silence.

From the shadows of the trees, Charles stepped forward. His royal coat gleamed in the sunlight, and behind him stood a line of armed soldiers.

He smiled coldly.

"Well, well, look who is back." Said Charles holding his bloody knife. Well done, Nika. You've saved me the trouble of finding it myself."

Behind him, Lorenzo's crew lay scattered across the sand—lifeless, broken. Charles's soldiers had cut them down like cattle.

"You vile, nasty devil!" Lorenzo roared, charging forward. But before his blade could reach Charles, he was surrounded by redcoats.

"Taria—can you cast a spell?" Nika whispered, scanning for escape.

"Not here," Taria answered, panic flickering in her eyes. "I need water, I'm too far from the ocean."

At that exact moment, the sea itself rose up. With a thunderous crash, Hylos emerged, towering and furious. A wave swept across the beach, tearing half of Charles's men from their feet and dragging them screaming into the tide.

"Run-now!" Hylos bellowed.

Charles lunged, seizing Nika by her hair. "The book— give it to me!"

Nika twisted, defiant. She raised the book high over his head, her eyes flashing with fire. "You want the secret? Then take it!"

With all her strength, she slammed the heavy tome against his skull. Charles staggered, blood streaming down his temple.

Nika dived into the sea. "Captain—I'm sorry for your loss," she whispered to Lorenzo as the waves swallowed them.

"Follow me!" Hylos ordered, his voice rumbling like thunder.

As they fled, Lorenzo's rage boiled over. "How did Charles know of the Temple? Of the book? What in Zeus's name happened aboard his ship, Nika?"

While they cut through the waves, Nika told the story— her lost crew, their betrayal, Charles's manipulation, and his hunger for the Temple's power.

"So he sails with your men now?" Lorenzo grown.

"Yes. He knows me. Too well now."

Santigo swam closer, gasping for breath. "Then where are we going?"

Nika's eyes glowed faintly in the moonlight. "To Iota. A pirate town. There we'll find a ship. An old friend owes me one."

At her words, Hylos halted, his expression grave.

"I'll return to Atlantis. Father must know you seek the Temple of the Seven Seas," he said.

"Go, brother," Taria whispered. "I'll stay."

With that, Hylos vanished into the dark waves.

Part IV: The Earth and the Alliance

Chapter 22: The Betrayal of Shira

Two hours later, lanterns appeared in the mist. The lawless spires of Iota rose before them, jagged silhouettes against a restless sky, flickering with firelight. The town seemed alive with chaos—music spilled from taverns, drunken laughter echoed in alleys, dice clattered across tables, and somewhere in the distance, the shriek of a fight broke out.

"So where's this friend of yours?" Lorenzo muttered, his hand never far from his saber as he scanned the cutthroats stumbling along the pier.

"Shira," Nika replied. "He runs the theater."

The word theater sounded almost out of place in such a den of thieves, but they followed her regardless. They weaved through streets sticky with spilled ale and sawdust, past brawlers and card-sharps, until a great wooden theater came into view. Its doors spilled with torchlight and noise, the sign above cracked but still bold: The House of Dreams.

Inside, an audience roared with laughter as a man on stage spun a tale. His presence filled the room; his booming voice held the crowd like a captain commands his crew.

"Shira, Shira—tell us again how you became master of this theater!" someone shouted, tankard sloshing.

"With pleasure!" the man thundered, strutting across the boards. "Even when I was a kid, I loved to play into pirates with my friends. I thought childhood would last forever, but then dad sent me to school. Studying was very difficult for me, and I often ran away from classes. Soon dad died. We had nowhere to get money. I had to quit my studies and go work in a factory to somehow feed us. I worked hard and earned very little, we barely made ends meet. So, several years passed. I was always very tired, we still lived very poor, and the situation didn't change.

Something had to be done. The road to my factory passed by the theater, and I often saw how well-dressed cheerful people coming out of it. And then I accidentally met one of the actors who offered me a small part-time job in the theater, he needed a loader. That's how it went. Suddenly—I belonged not to the machines, but to the theater! From loader, to actor, to master of this house! And here I stand—lord of dreams!"

His words rolled like poetry, half-truth, half-lie, but delivered with such fire that even the drunkest sailor leaned forward to listen. When he finished, the crowd erupted, pounding mugs on tables, stamping their boots in approval.

Shira bowed deeply. "Now, a musical interlude! Drink, laugh, and when I return—I shall sing again!"

The audience roared as he swept offstage, vanishing into the curtains.

Nika followed, her steps measured, heart cautious. Lorenzo and the others lingered at the door, eyes sharp, hands resting on hilts.

"Shira," Nika said warmly, stepping into the dressing room where faded costumes hung like ghosts. "How many winters have passed! It is good to see you."

He turned—and his eyes widened in delight. "Nika! Hero of the seas! You are alive!" His arms enveloped her in a theatrical embrace. "How are things, girl?"

"Good enough," she replied with a faint smile, though her eyes betrayed exhaustion.

Shira chuckled, but his gaze narrowed. "I doubt it. Heroes never come to me with good tidings. What brings you here?"

"I need your Matilda. Just for a while. I'll return her, I swear it."

"A ship?" he echoed, tilting his head. "From me? No problem. But first—you look half-starved. Sit. Eat. Rest."

Her body ached from storms and sleepless nights. For a moment, a warm meal felt like mercy. She lowered herself into the chair, breathing out.

Behind her, Shira moved to the cabinet. His hands sifted through masks, velvet cloaks, and false crowns—until they found a hidden drawer of iron. Slowly, he slid it open. His fingers curled around the smooth handle of a cudgel.

"Thank you, Shira," Nika said softly, unaware, her eyes fixed on the table.

"Always for you," he murmured.

The swing came sharp and sudden. Pain blossomed, the world tilted, and the world went black, she felt unconscious.

Chapter 23: The Chase of the Green Lily

The theater smelled of sweat, rum, and betrayal. Nika rubbed the back of her head, still dizzy from Shira's treachery. Her hands clenched.

"I swear on the seas, he won't get away with this," she muttered.

But they had no time to linger—Charles had the book, the crystal, and a head start.

Outside, the streets of Iota were chaos. Torches lit the muddy alleys in a dull orange glow, and Charles's men swaggered through the crowds with their red coats, dragging Nika's stolen prize.

"There they are," Lorenzo hissed, pointing towards the pier.

Nika didn't hesitate. She broke into a sprint, boots pounding the cobblestones, cloak billowing like a storm. Taria and Santigo followed, but Nika was already too fast—like a shadow, she closed in.

"Stop them!" one of Charles's men barked.

Three soldiers turned, blades flashing.

Nika leapt forward, grabbed the first by his collar, and smashed her forehead into his nose—blood sprayed, and he fell like a sack of stones. She twisted aside as the second swung his cutlass, caught his wrist mid-air, and yanked—his blade flew free. In the same motion, she spun and slammed the hilt into his jaw.

"Who's next?" she growled.

The third charged, musket raised. Nika ducked low, slid across the wet cobblestones, and kicked his legs out. The man toppled, his musket clattering harmlessly away. Nika rose with predatory grace, her eyes burning.

"Pathetic," she spat.

Taria caught up, panting, her eyes wide. "You—beat three men in seconds."

Nika smirked. "That was just the warm-up."

The streets of Iota turned into a chase. Charles's soldiers tried to slow them, but Nika cut through the ranks like a tempest—dodging, striking, disarming, each movement as fluid as water, as sharp as fire. Every blow was calculated, elegant, brutal. The townsfolk gasped, some cheering, some ducking for cover.

By the time they reached the docks, a dozen redcoats lay groaning in the mud.

"There!" Santigo pointed. A ship with dark sails—Matilda—rocked gently at the pier.

Nika vaulted aboard first, hand already gripping the wheel. "Everyone, move! Now!"

Lorenzo shoved Taria and Santigo up the gangplank. The moment his boots hit deck, Nika shouted:

"Raise anchor—set sail before Charles realizes what's happened!"

The sails snapped open, catching the midnight wind. Matilda groaned, then surged forward, cutting through the black waters of the Amazon mouth.

Later that night, Nika sat cross-legged in the captain's cabin. She held the torn page of the book in one hand, her eyes narrowing as she read aloud:

"Behind the big river, behind the damp hills, after the fourth rain, the fourth month... there will be the kingdom small, and you will not confuse it with anything else. A kingdom called Little Lily."

"Charles will be there," Taria whispered, staring out at the endless jungle looming over the riverbanks.

"Where is this place—Little Lily?" Santigo asked, brow furrowed.

Taria turned slowly, her voice low and serious. "The elves. The hidden kingdom of the Amazon elves."

Nika's lips curled into a grin. "Then Charles won't stand a chance without this page." She tapped the parchment, eyes gleaming. "And we have it."

At that very moment, Lorenzo, squinting from the bow, shouted: "Sail ahead—Charles's ship!"

The moonlight revealed the British frigate, its silhouette dark against the jungle canopy.

Nika's grin widened, fierce and merciless. "Perfect. Let him chase shadows. We'll be with the elves before he even knows where to look."

She folded the page carefully and tucked it inside her vest. Then, to her crew:

"Stay sharp. The hunt for the Green Lily has begun."

Chapter 24: The Ghost in the Shadows

The Matilda cut silently through the black river waters, its sails ghostlike under the moon. Ahead, Charles's frigate glowed with lantern light, anchored like a predator waiting in the dark.

…How, did this bastard knew about the location? He did not had the torn page?

Nika stood at the prow, eyes sharp. "The book and crystal are in his cabin. I'll get them back."

"You'll be walking into a lion's den," Lorenzo warned.

Nika smirked. "Then let the lion beware."

In the blink of an eye, her body shrank, fur sprouting, until a mouse leapt to the rope lines and scurried unseen towards the frigate.

Inside Charles's cabin, the air was heavy with sweat and anger.

"Do you know where the kingdom of elves is?" Charles barked, pacing like a caged beast.

Ios shifted nervously. "We were here years ago, but only the witch knows the path."

Charles slammed his fist onto the table, rattling the lantern. "Think, or I'll toss you to the river monsters!"

Alex and Lucas remained silent, eyes lowered.

None noticed the small mouse creeping onto the table. None saw it shimmer, stretch, and rise into the shape of Nika Kassia. Saber in one hand, she snatched the book and crystal with the other.

"Looking for these?" she said coolly.

"Witch!" Charles bellowed, snatching his sword.

Two guards burst in with muskets. Nika was already moving—she flipped over the table, slicing a candle in half. Hot wax splattered the first guard's eyes, and he screamed. She spun low, cut the strap of the second guard's scabbard, then slammed her boot into his chest, sending him crashing into the wall.

Alex, Lucas, and Ios froze. "It's her..." whispered Lucas.

Nika's glare burned through them. "Traitors. Stay out of my way, or I'll carve the truth out of your cowardly hearts."

Charles roared and lunged. Their blades clashed, steel ringing in the confined space.

The duel was vicious.

Charles fought like a storm, heavy strikes crashing down with brute strength. Each blow rattled Nika's arms, forcing her back. She ducked one swing—his blade embedded into the oak desk, splitting it in half.

Nika darted left, struck with a flurry, but Charles parried and countered with a slash that nicked her shoulder.

She hissed, retreating a step. "Not bad... for a pompous prince."

"You're slower than I remember," Charles sneered. "Your power makes you weak."

"Or maybe you're too blind to see the trick coming."

She lunged, feinted high, then swept low, kicking his legs out. Charles stumbled but didn't fall—he caught himself on the wall and slammed his elbow into her ribs. The air whooshed out of her chest.

Pain flared, but Nika gritted her teeth, rolled aside, and caught the falling lantern midair. With a wicked grin, she hurled it at Charles. Flames exploded across the cabin wall, forcing him back.

"You witch!" he roared through smoke.

Nika leapt onto the table, the book and crystal glowing in her arms. "I told you before, Charles... ghosts don't burn."

With one last smirk, she vanished in a flash of white light.

On the Matilda, Lorenzo, Taria, and Santigo held their breath.

"Signal, signal..." Santigo muttered.

Then—a flare of ghostly fire arced above Charles's ship.

"There's our sign!" Lorenzo barked.

Nika appeared in the water beside them, clutching the book and crystal tight. "Follow me—swim for the elves!" she ordered, her voice fierce.

They dove into the black river, cutting through the current, while behind them Charles stormed onto his deck, eyes blazing with fury.

"Find her! Tear this river apart if you must!" His roar shook the night.

But the White Ghost was already gone, swallowed by shadows of the Amazon.

Chapter 25: The Whisper

"I see another ship, captain."

Charles saw Nika's ship and they decided to storm into it, that result destroying the whole ship.

"I know where she is…" said Charles. "Follow my command."

Floating along the river, Nika's team hit the waterfall.

"Captain—" she began, but it was too late.

The water dropped away beneath them. For one endless heartbeat, they were weightless, flying. Then— CRASH!

Nika tumbled into the depths, fighting for breath. Salt and river mud filled her mouth, and in the chaos she could barely see where Lorenzo, Santigo, or Taria were.

"Swim!" she screamed, though her voice was drowned by the torrent.

Bodies crashed against rocks. For a moment it seemed the current would tear them apart. Then, coughing and clawing, one by one, they dragged themselves onto the muddy bank. Nika collapsed on her knees, her chest heaving. Beside her, Lorenzo cursed, spitting river water. Taria lay half in, half out of the water, her gills fluttering as she gasped for air.

The world spun. Above them, mist from the fallen painted rainbows across the air. The forest beyond glowed faintly with its own light.

And there—watching silently—stood the elves.

They were slight, their hair pale as moonlight, their eyes reflecting green like forest leaves. Their movements were quick, cautious, like deer ready to vanish at the crack of a twig.

One elf darted off at lightning speed, disappearing between the trees. Moments later he returned, leading another. Taller, older, dressed in emerald robes that shimmered with threads of gold. His presence made even the mist still.

"Brother Urik, we saw people from the waterfall," whispered one of the elves.

Urik's gaze swept across them, pausing on Nika. "Four... one human girl, one sea-born princess, and two pirates. Hm." His eyes are narrowed. "I know this girl."

Nika staggered to her feet, brushing mud from her clothes. Despite her soaked hair clinging to her face, she smiled.

"Urik," she said breathlessly, her voice breaking between coughs, "how many years have we not seen each other!"

He blinked, started. Then his sternness broke into laughter. "Nika Kassia... the White Ghost herself, crawling out of my river like a drowned rat." He stepped forward and embraced her tightly.

The elves murmured in surprise, exchanging glances.

"Welcome to the Green Lily," Urik said warmly. "You've survived the fall, and that means the forest has allowed you entry. Few can say the same."

Lorenzo muttered, still dripping, "If this is a welcome, I'd hate to see a rejection."

Urik turned his gaze on him, unamused. "Pirate tongues should be silent in these woods."

"Ha! That'll be the day," Lorenzo shot back.

Nika cut between them. "Please, Urik. We didn't come here to fight. We need your help."

The elf leader studied her for a long moment, then gestured. "Come. You've had a hard road. Sit at our table. Tell me everything."

And so they followed him into the heart of the Green Lily.

Chapter 26: The Betrayal

"Tell me why you came, my friend" said Urik, inviting Nika and her team to sit down at the table, relax and have lunch.

"Your road was long and hard to get here." Urik said.

Nika told the whole story of her adventures.

After listening attentively to Nika's story, Urik said:

"No wonder they are looking for us. Mother Nature will help us hide from them. If what is said in the book is true, and you already have the first crystal, it turns out that you are chosen one, which means you can finish the work you have begun."

"First, Urik, let's find the green crystal." Nika said, leafing through the book.

"Well, what does it say?" Taria asked.

"Beyond the Green Lily hills, you will find a tree, unusual, like their inhabitants. And talking to Mother Nature, under it, you will find your second key."

"Another nonsense." Lorenzo snorted.

"In this forest there are different trees, both large and small, and thick and thin." Taria said.

"It is possible that there is a tree in the field of view that has magical powers like elves." Nika suggested.

"Or a tree as thin and small as elves." Taria agreed.

"Start the search, immediately." said Urik. "Mother Nature will tell you where to go. In the meantime, Nika, give me the crystal and the book, I'll hide them in a safe place."

Everyone scattered into the forest, eager to seek the mysterious tree. Taria guided a group toward the hills, while Lorenzo and Santigo discussed which direction was "smarter." Only Nika stayed behind. She felt in her bones that the answer was not where others were searched.

She slipped quietly into the deep forest, her boots sinking into the moss. The canopy whispered with voices, old and patient, the language of roots and leaves.

Closing her eyes, she whispered into the silence:

"Spirits of Mother Nature, help me find the second key. Spirits of the land, guide me to your treasure."

At first, there was nothing but wind. Then—soft, crimson petals burst from the ground at her feet. Red poppies unfurled in a line, glowing faintly in the forest glow, forming a path.

Nika's eyes widened. "Thank you..."

She followed the ribbon of poppies deeper into the woods. Soon, she stood before an odd sight: a slender, stunted tree, shaped almost like an elf. It had no branches, no crown of leaves, no birdsong perched on its boughs, not even ants crawling on its bark. It stood bare and alone, unnatural in its stillness.

"Something's wrong here..." Nika whispered, circling it.

Her instincts were right. The tree was no tree at all, but a vessel, a hollow shell crafted to guard something ancient.

Kneeling, Nika pressed her palm to the earth.

"Mother Nature, hear me. Give me the second key."

The ground trembled. The air thickened with the scent of soil and moss. From the shadows of the forest, a colossal

90

figure rose—made of roots and stone, eyes glowing emerald. The Spirit of Earth.

Nika leapt back in awe, her heart hammering.

The Spirit bent down, reached into the false tree, and drew out a glowing green crystal. Holding it in hands vast as boulders, the Spirit lowered it into Nika's waiting palms.

The moment she touched it, the world dissolved—the Spirit, the tree, even the poppies. Everything vanished into mist. She stood alone, clutching the crystal that pulsed with living power.

"Another key... the second step." Nika's lips curved into a tired but joyful smile.

She ran back to the village, her heart light with triumph.

But when she arrived, her joy turned to ice.

The Green Lily was in ruins. Houses burned half to ash. Wooden bridges cracked and broken. The ground was littered with the still forms of elves, their lifeless eyes staring at the sky.

"No..." Nika whispered, staggering forward. "This… this can't be."

Her knees buckled. She clutched the green crystal tighter, as if it could anchor her against the horror.

"Urik..." she choked out.

Her breath hitched as her mind raced. Only one name fits this massacre.

"Charles..." Nika's eyes blazed, tears mixing with fury. "Charles, I am going to kill you!"

She ran towards the river, the jungle tearing at her arms and clothes, her blood singing with rage. At the shore, sails loomed in the mist—a British frigate, Charles's banner flying high.

She clenched her fist. Then, with a breath, she vanished. Her form shimmered and dissolved into nothing. The White Ghost had become invisible.

Chapter 27: Wrath of the White Ghost

Silent as death, she teleported straight onto Charles's ship.

There were elves and her team, bound in iron shackles, forced to kneel like prisoners on the deck. Charles stood with his men, a bloody knife still in his hand, speaking low to his officers.

"She will come," Charles said coldly. "The witch will not abandon her crew."

Urik spat blood onto the boards. "You will be punished for your crime!"

"Shut up before you die," Lucas sneered, kicking him to the floor.

Nika clenched her fists. Her voice rank out like thunder:

"Spirits of the earth, hear me! Birds, peck the villains. Alligators, rise from the depths. Wasps, sting them to death!"

The sky darkened. The river boiled. A storm of wings and claws descended as shrieking gulls and ravens attacked the crew, tearing at their eyes. Alligators surged against the hull, dragging screaming sailors into the current. From the creeping vines written like living snakes, wrapping around muskets and throats.

"Cut them free!" Ios screamed, hacking at the vines, but the more they cut, the faster they grew back, re-knitting like flesh.

The deck turned into chaos. Steel clashed against claw, men shrieked, the air reeked of salt, sweat, and blood. For two endless hours the battle rages, until only a handful of Charles's men still stood, trembling and broken.

Then came the roar.

From nothing, a tigress leapt onto the deck, eyes burning like twin suns. She slashed with claws, tearing through armor as if it were paper. Pirates dropped their blades and fled overboard, screaming into the black water.

"It's her! The witch—kill her!" Charles bellowed, though his voice cracked with fear.

The tigress shimmered, fur melting into skin. Nika stood in her place, saber flashing in her hand.

"Release my friends," she commanded, "or you'll wish you had drowned with the others."

Before Charles could answer, Alex lunged, pressing a blade to Taria's throat.

"Try it," he hissed. "One move, and she dies."

Charles stepped forward. "Give us the book. Give us the crystals."

Nika's eyes are narrowed. Slowly, she lowered her saber to the deck, crouching as if defeated. Her hand dipped into her pocket. "Let them go first. Then you'll have what you want."

Charles smirked, stepping closer.

Too close.

Nika whipped her hand forward—out flew not the crystals, but a fireball blazing like the heart of a forge. It exploded at Charles's feet, throwing him backward. Smoke and fire swallowed the deck.

"Now!" Nika roared. Creepers burst from the planks, binding Charles and Alex in coils of living rope. They are thrashed and cursed, but the vines squeezed tighter.

Exhaustion struck her like a hammer—her vision blurred, knees buckled. Still, she stumbled to the iron cage, pressed her hand against the lock. The metal glowed red-hot, then melted like wax. The shackles fell, her friends and the elves scrambling free.

Nika collapsed onto the deck, too weak to move.

Urik rushed to her side, pulling a vial of shimmering green liquid from his cloak. He dripped three drops onto her brow, whispered words older than stone, and laid his hand upon her head. A glow spread, her breath steadied, and color returned to her face.

"She lives," Urik said.

Lorenzo lifted Nika gently in his arms. Together, the elves and the survivors slipped back into the riverboats and rowed for the hidden village. Behind them, Charles's ship smoldered, the cries of his bound men fading into the night.

Urik raised his voice as they reached the shore:

"She must rest. Tomorrow, we honor the fallen with burial, and tomorrow night we feast for our survival."

The elves answered with a mournful song, carrying the dead away by torchlight, while the White Ghost slept, cradled in the arms of those she had saved.

Chapter 28: Grief and Feast

The next day dawned soft and pale, as if the forest itself mourned. Mist curled through the green hills, and the elves moved silently, carrying their fallen on carved wooden biers. They laid the bodies in the roots of ancient trees, whispering prayers in a tongue older than man. Each elf pressed a hand to the earth, returning the souls of their kin to Mother Nature.

 "From root to blossom, from blossom to seed, we are never gone." Urik said quietly.

That night, the silence of grief gave way to the roar of life. Fires blazed high in the center of the elven village. Long tables of polished oak were laden with fruits shining like jewels, roasted boar, breads shaped like lilies, and cups brimming with silver wine that glowed faintly in the torchlight.

Urik stood and raised a carved horn.

"Brothers, sisters, tonight we honor the brave—those who fell, and those who still fight. Raise your cups to the White Ghost, who called storm and claw to save us!"

The elves roared in answer, their voices like a forest alive. They danced in spirals, sang their ancient songs, and filled the night with the thrum of drums and the piercing cry of flutes.

By the next evening, the festival is still lingered. The elves had begun to laugh again, to play, to pass dishes of vegetables and fruits and honeyed wine beneath the torchlight. Santigo could not stop eating, peeling his plate with berries and roasted roots, while Taria and Lorenzo waited patiently outside Urik's oak-tree dwelling for Nika to wake.

Eventually, the door creaked open. Nika stepped out from the high wooden stairs, the morning light catching her pale hair. Her eyes were tired but steady. From below, Taria spotted her instantly.

"Come down, we're here!" she called, running up the steps before Nika could even descend. She threw her arms around her and hugged her tightly.

"Taria... what happened? Don't worry, I'm fine," Nika whispered with a faint smile.

"Nothing at all," Taria said, still holding her. "You just saved us, like always. You only needed the rest."

"How do you feel?" Lorenzo asked, crossing his arms but with concern in his eyes.

"Very well, Lorenzo. Thank you for asking," Nika replied warmly.

Taria then told her everything—the battle, the vines, the terror on the ship, and how Urik healed her with the potion of holy water and whispered spells.

When she finished, Nika approached Urik, who stood near the fire where the elves danced. She bowed her head gratefully.

"Thank you, Urik. I owe you."

The elf leader placed a hand on her shoulder. "You are our *talyon saro*," he said solemnly in his language.

"What does that mean?" Lorenzo asked, curious.

"It means 'our fearless warrior,'" Nika explained softly. "That's what Urik called me the very first time we met."

The elves cheered and clapped as Urik raised his voice: "Let it be known—the White Ghost has earned her name among us!"

The music swelled again, and elves pulled Nika into the circle of dancers. Flames lit the night, sparks flying like stars. Even Lorenzo, after much grumbling, was handed a horn of glowing wine and ended up laughing as the elves pulled him into the rhythm.

Santigo leaned back against a tree, wiping juice from his chin. "Nika, tell us," he said between bites, "how did you first meet the elves?"

The firelight flickered in Nika's eyes. She smiled faintly, remembering.

"It was a long time ago..."

And as the feast carried on, she began to tell the story of her first encounter with the Green Lily.

Chapter 29: The Story of Black Beard

"It was November, and I was with my old team far to the North. The winds there cut like knives, and the sea itself seemed made of ice. We had gone to help the Vikings— building them ships and bringing them what food we could. That winter was harsher than any they had seen in decades. The ground was buried in snow, the rivers frozen. They had almost nothing to eat, and in desperation they turned to us for aid.

I managed to buy furs in Turkey to keep them warm, but food was the greater struggle. It was not just about finding it—it was keeping it fresh. Ships then had no way to preserve supplies for long voyages. Meat rotted, bread molded, fruit soured before we reached our destination. We needed something more, something miraculous, if we were to keep the Vikings alive through the winter.

One night, as I sat in a dim tavern, staring into my mug and wondering how in heaven I could solve this problem, I overheard a pair of pirates at the next table. Their words struck me like lightning. They were whispering about a magical place hidden on the Amazon River. A forest overflowing with food of every kind—fruits, grains, spices—and, they claimed, once taken from that place, the food never spoiled.

It was exactly what I needed. The only obstacle was finding it. They spoke in low voices, full of fear, for they said the forest was cursed, guarded by spirits who devoured men that dared step into their land. But I was not afraid of curses. The true challenge, as I saw it, was to learn where this place was. And that, as you might guess, was simple enough. A few bottles of rum, a few careless laughs, and before the night was over their tongues were loose. By morning, the coordinates of that mysterious place were in my pocket.

I wasted no time. At dawn, I set sail for the Amazon. But fate has a way of testing us when we are certain of our path. On that journey, we crossed paths with a ship flying black sails, its flag stitched with a death's head. It was Captain Black Beard himself.

Lorenzo interrupted me then, his face pale. 'I don't believe it.'

'Black Beard?' Santiago said, shaking his head. 'He's the most furious pirate in the world. You can't even look at him and come away alive.'

"I only smiled at their fear and drew from beneath my cloak this copper medallion, strung on a chain. A compass was engraved upon it, still shining though it had seen a hundred storms."

The firelight danced across the medallion in Nika's hands.

"Then what is this?" I asked them.

Lorenzo gasped. "It can't be... that was Black Beard's medallion."

"Yes," I said. "So let me finish my tale. I knew at once he was not prowling those waters for any good cause. I slipped into invisibility, stole across the waves, and boarded his ship unseen. From the shadows I listened to his crew. Black Beard had taken a commission from the King of Spain. The old king was decrepit, bent with sickness and greed, too weak to stand yet too stubborn to surrender his throne. He had heard of the elves—beings who lived for centuries, kept young by the secret of living water. The king, desperate for more years to hoard his treasures, had sent Black Beard to hunt them down. And for gold, Black Beard would sail into the devil's mouth itself.

When I heard this, I knew I could not waste time. I had to find the elves before he did, to warn them, to keep their secret safe. So, I turned my ship upriver, deeper and deeper into the Amazon. The journey was long, days upon days of winding currents, roaring rapids, and endless jungle on every side. My crew grew up. Supplies dwindled. The men began to despair.

We did not know if the elves even existed, nor where to find them. The forest loomed over us like a living wall, and still no sign came. It seemed hopeless.

But destiny has its own timing. And just when everyone seemed lost...However, as always, with God's help. Or was it the destiny?

Anyway..

The weather was glorious that day, the kind of morning that feels as if the world itself has paused to breathe. The sun shimmered across the water, warm but gentle, while dragonflies hovered in glimmering swarms, darting over the river like sparks. Birds sang from the canopy in a hundred different voices—whistles, trills, low coos—all blending into a strange, enchanting chorus.

It was then that one of those curious birds, a bright little fellow with feathers like emerald fire, decided to take a special interest in Lucas. It flew right up to him, flapping over his head as he struggled with the helm. He muttered curses, tried to shake it off—but the bird refused to leave.

The crew, of course, found this endlessly amusing. Every few seconds the bird would swoop down and tug a lock of his hair, or peck at his shoulder, or hover so close Lucas nearly crossed his eyes. Finally, in a fury, Lucas abandoned the helm altogether, tore off his boot, and began chasing the bird in wild circles across the deck, swinging the boot like a weapon.

The rest of us spilled onto the deck, laughter roaring as we watched him wage war against a creature no larger than a fist. He stumbled, waved, cursed, and the bird chirped as though mocking him. In the commotion, everyone forgot the steering wheel. No one noticed the current quickening beneath us.

It was only minutes later when Santiago shouted, "The river bends ahead!"—but it was too late.

The ship spined. The water roared. And then, like a stone tossed into the sky, we plunged over the edge of a waterfall.

The world turned into spray and thunder. I remember the crash, the weightless moment as though the river itself had vanished beneath us, and then the brutal impact. Somehow, we survived. Bruised, soaked, gasping—but alive.

When I woke up, my wrists and ankles were bound with rope. Around us stood figures both terrible and magnificent. They were not men, not quite. They were elves, their eyes sharp as blades, their movements silent as shadows. Their bows glimmered with runes, their clothes woven from living vines.

One of them stood above me—the leader, tall, grim, his gaze so fierce I thought he meant to strike me down where I lay. This was Urik. His face was carved from stone, his voice low as thunder when he spoke.

I tried to reason with him. "If you don't listen, if you don't hurry—pirates will find you. They will capture your strongest, destroy the rest."

At first, Urik only laughed, a short, cutting laugh that echoed like steel against stone. He told me humans always lied, always begged. But he also had the strange gift of reading hearts, and when his eyes lingered on mine, he saw the truth. He spared us—not because he feared us, but because he decided we were no threat.

But before long, my words proved themselves. The pirates came. Black Beard's crew found the elves' sanctuary and stormed upon it, blades flashing, muskets firing. The elves, caught by surprise, staggered at first.

I knew the battle would end in slaughter if Black Beard was not stopped. So, I vanished, slipping through the chaos invisible. I crept up behind him—he was bellowing orders, swinging his saber like a king of devils—and with all my strength I smashed him with a heavy iron object. He roared once and collapsed, unconscious at my feet.

That was when I saw it—the medallion hanging on his chest. Not just any medallion. This one was alive with power.

You ask why I took it?

Because this medallion was no simple trinket. Under the right conditions, it became a compass, a guide to anything its bearer sought. To everyone else, it was nothing but copper. But in the right hands—mine—it could point the way to destiny itself.

Meanwhile the battle rages. The elves fought like the forest itself had risen to defend them. Vines struck like whips, arrows flew like rain, roots split the earth beneath the pirates' feet. The pirates fought back savagely, but here, in the heart of the Green Lily forest, the elves were unbreakable. Soon Black Beard's men were overwhelmed, beaten, bound, dragged away as prisoners.

When the battle was over, Urik himself came to me. This time there was no laughter in him. He dropped to one knee, bowed his head, and spoke words I will never forget.

"From this day," he said, "you are one of us. Part of the Green Lily. For your courage, for your warning, and for saving our people—I give you the blessing of the elves. The power of nature, and the fulfillment of one wish."

I bowed in return, humbled, and spoke plainly: "Help me find the magical forest. A place where fruits and vegetables grow and stay fresh forever. A northern village depends on it—they are starving. This is all I ask."

Urik stared at me for a long moment, then laughed, but this time it was not cruel. It was full of wonder.

"Of all desires," he said, "gold, power, long life—you ask for food to feed the hungry. Truly, you are the strangest human I have ever met. You have a pure soul and a great heart. Our home will always be open to you."

He explained that the power he had given me—the magic of earth itself—was the key. He would teach me how to use it. And he did. With my crew beside me, we filled our ships with food beyond imagining. He showed me how to bless it, to preserve it so no rot would ever touch it.

And when at last it was time to part, Urik clasped my hands and spoke two words in Elvish: "*Talyon saro.*"

I asked what they meant.

He just smiled. "Fearless warrior."

Chapter 30: Leaving the Green Lily

"But what happened to Black Beard?" Lorenzo couldn't calm down, his eyes still wide in disbelief.

"Yes, everything is very simple," Nika said with a sly smile. "Urik approached him, cast his spell, lifted Black Beard's body high into the air, and sealed him inside a tree. His life force was returned to nature itself. Now he will serve the forest instead of plundering it." She chuckled softly. "Not such a bad ending for the world's most feared pirate, don't you think?"

Santigo leaned forward, curiosity gleaming in his eyes. "Then tell me, Nika... how did you get the ability to turn into animals?"

"In earth magic," Nika explained, "as in all the elemental magics, there are branches—skills."

"Skills?" Lorenzo frowned.

"Yes. Earth bending is not only about commanding soil and stone. It is about breathing life into plants, shaping roots and vines, moving mountains, and, yes... transformation. Earth grants the ability to shift into any living being, to borrow its form and strength."

Lorenzo rubbed his chin. "You mean to tell me... all four elements have hidden powers like this?"

"Exactly. For water—there's more than raising waves or freezing rivers. It's the gift to breathe underwater, to sing like sirens with voices that enchant, to swim with the speed of dolphins. Fire can summon storms of flame, but it can also purify, heal, and illuminate. Air grants flight, whispers across distances, even the bending of sound itself. Each element is more than people think."

Lorenzo squinted at her. "If you have all this, then why did you nearly die back on the ship? You should have been invincible."

Nika's expression grew tired, but her voice was calm. "Because one power is light, easy to carry. But if you use many at once—strength, invisibility, transformations, vines, storms—your life energy is drained. It takes time to restore. And that night, I spent more than I had to give."

Her words hung heavy. You could see Lorenzo wasn't satisfied—his lips pressed tight—but he didn't argue further.

That night, the crew found their beds under the emerald boughs of the Green Lily forest. The air smelled of moss and sweet flowers, and for a moment it seemed as though peace had returned.

But peace never lasts.

By morning, Urik handed them a woven satchel, strong as steel despite its roots and bark. "For the book and the crystals," he said. "So long as it is bound in this bag, no thief can see it, and no spell can sense it."

They thanked him, and soon after, aboard the British ship they had claimed, Nika and her companions set out once more on the hunt for the next crystal.

Meanwhile...

Far back in the Amazon, Charles and his men stirred. The vines that had once strangled them now lay limp, brittle as dry grass. The spell had faded with time.

They rose from the wreckage, battered but unbroken.

"Captain, what do we do now? We have no weapons, no ship," Ios muttered, glaring at the steaming jungle.

Charles's face twisted in rage. His pride was more wounded than his body. "We build. From the bones of the broken hull, we lash a raft. We get to Iota. We take a ship, and then—we hunt her. Nika will not escape me again."

His crew nodded grimly, gathering wood as Charles's fury burned brighter than the sun above.

Aboard Nika's ship…

The air was heavy as Nika turned the crackling pages of the book. Strange letters glowed faintly, shifting like sand in the wind. She read aloud:

"What could be more beautiful than painting with sand? Crossing the floor of the world, on the edge of it, there will be an abyss full of serpents that devour fire. And when you step into it, you will be doomed to eternal sleep. There you will find the next key..."

"This book amazes me once again with its nonsense," Santiago muttered, rolling his eyes.

Lorenzo slammed a fist against the railing. "Well? Where do we go now?"

Nika's eyes lit suddenly, her voice a whisper of excitement. "Abyss... sand... serpents... eternal sleep. Oh, I know where we are sailing. To the dragons."

Silence. Then Lorenzo groaned, dragging his hands down his face.

"Dragons?" he barked. "Dios mío! A fine plan. We'll all be roasted like chickens. Santiago and I will be served for

106

lunch, you witch for dinner, and you, Princess, for dessert!"

Taria laughed softly and placed a hand on his shoulder. "Do not fear, Captain. Dragons are not what the stories tell. They are ancient and wise—kind and hospitable if you come with respect."

Lorenzo scowled, muttering curses, but his eyes betrayed his fear.

The sails caught the wind. The river widened, opening into an endless horizon. And so, the hunt for the crystal led them now... into the lands of fire and wings.

Part V: The Fire and Abyss

Chapter 31: Unknown Island

Maybe it is the destiny or the unknown path but sometimes things happen. Unpredictable...

"Lorenzo, stop grumbling, we're going to Egypt — to new adventures," Nika said, her eyes sparkling with stubborn fire.

"Nika, in what order did you receive the four elements of magic?" Taria suddenly asked.

"Water, earth, fire, and air," Nika answered without hesitation.

"Don't you think it's strange," Taria leaned closer, her voice low, "that in the book the crystals appear in the exact same order?"

Nika's gaze grew distant. "I understand what you mean, but maybe it's just coincidence." She turned, heading toward her cabin.

"I don't think so," Taria replied, following. "I want to talk to you."

"Alright, talk," Nika said, pausing at the doorway.

"You know that in the Temple of the Seven Seas you can make any wish to the gods, and it will immediately come true," the princess whispered.

"Yes, I know about the desire," Nika answered, her voice heavy. "But I still don't know what I want. Before, I only dreamed of finding the temple. I thought once I found it, I could study all the secrets of the world. Now... all I wish is to bring my team back, and restore their trust in me. But I don't want the temple to force them to forgive. I want them to realize themselves, how wrong they were. Only then... maybe I'd forgive. But the truth is," her voice cracked, "I miss them terribly."

Taria's face softened. "My father once told me: if there is a wall of corals before you, and you see no road, find the gap in the wall and break it. Then the path will open."

"Thanks, Taria." Nika exhaled, half a smile on her lips. "You wanted to talk only about the temple, or is there something more serious?"

"I have an offer," Taria said carefully. "Maybe you will fulfill Zack's wish."

"What wish?"

"He knows we are sailing to the temple. He told me he would love to be human again."

"Human? Again?" Nika's eyebrows knitted. "Why would he suddenly want to be human?"

"I'll tell you my story," Taria began softly. "Listen carefully, and you will understand everything..."

But before she could continue, the heavens split.

Dark clouds rolled in from nowhere, swallowing the stars. The wind shrieked like banshees. Waves slammed against the ship's hull with monstrous force. The mast groaned and snapped like a twig.

The crew rushed to ropes and sails, shouting over the roar of the storm. Lightning split the night, turning the ocean white.

"By the gods! She's breaking apart!" Lorenzo bellowed, clutching the wheel as the ship shuddered. "This is your fault, witch! Every curse comes from you!"

The deck split under their feet. Water swallowed the hold. The storm seized the ship like a toy and hurled it against the waves.

One final crack split the vessel in two. Nika screamed an order, but it was drowned in thunder. The sea claimed them.

When the sun rose, it was merciless and blinding.

On the shore of a deserted island, four figures lay scattered in the sand like wreckage.

Nika stirred first, coughing seawater from her lungs. Her hair was plastered to her face, her clothes torn by rocks and waves. Nearby, Santiago groaned and rolled onto his back, muttering prayers to every saint he knew.

Lorenzo was already awake, pacing and cursing at the horizon. His clothes hung in tatters, his face red with fury. "Damn it, Witch! Every time! Every blasted time you lead us straight into death!" He kicked a piece of driftwood so hard it flew into the waves.

"Captain, enough," Nika rasped, pushing herself to her feet. "We survived. That's what matters."

"Survived?" Lorenzo spat. "We're stranded in the middle of nowhere! No food, no water, no ship! Dios mío, you'll get us killed before Egypt ever sees our sails."

Taria, still pale and shaken, knelt by the shore, cupping her hands to the water. With calm grace, she coaxed fish into her palms, pulling them to shore. "We will not starve," she said quietly.

Nika brushed sand from her arms, her eyes already on the dense green forest beyond the beach. "I'll search inland. Maybe there are villagers here, someone who can help us rebuild or guide us off this island."

She turned, her figure straight despite the exhaustion. "Stay here. Regain your strength. I'll be back."

With that, the White Ghost vanished into the trees, leaving the broken remnants of her crew to wait — and wonder if fate had thrown them into another trap.

The forest loomed before her, wild and untamed. The air was thick with the scent of damp leaves and strange flowers, their petals glowing faintly like embers in the dusk. Every step Nika took sank into moss, soft but unreal, softening her footsteps as if the island itself wished to swallow sound.

"Somewhere here, someone lives," she whispered to herself. "I can feel it."

The deeper she went, the more alive the forest became. Eyes glimmered in the shadows - monkeys, lizards, and creatures she could not name. Bright parrots screeched from the treetops, their cries echoing like warnings.

At one point, she reached a clearing where the ground was littered with cracked shells and bones. A circle of totems carved from black wood stood around it, their faces twisted into sneers and grimaces. The air felt heavy, pressing down on her shoulders.

"Witchcraft," Nika muttered, tightening her grip on the saber at her side. "Or a warning."

She pressed on. The forest resisted her, branches clutching her hair, roots rising like serpents to trip her steps. She didn't fail. She had walked through darker places before.

Finally, she heard it - voices. Human voices.

Nika crouched low, moving silently through the brush until she reached a ridge overlooking another clearing. Below, a group of villagers sat around a fire, their faces painted with streaks of red and white. Spears and bows rested at their sides. Children played near the flames, while older women ground herbs into clay bowls.

Relief washed through her. People. Civilization.

But it didn't last.

At the edge of the firelight, tied to a post, hung another man - not one of her crew. His skin was bruised, his shirt torn, his head slumped forward. Clearly, he was a prisoner.

"Not good," Nika whispered.

She watched as one of the villagers rose—tall, scarred across the cheek, wearing a necklace of animal teeth. He spoke in a guttural language Nika could barely follow. The others nodded, their eyes gleaming as if some grim decision had been made.

Nika felt the hairs on her arms rise. She didn't need to understand their words to know the meaning.

Sacrifice.

Her grip tightened on her saber. She could leave, return to her crew with news. Or she could do what she had always done: plunge headfirst into danger for the sake of a stranger.

The White Ghost did not hesitate.

Sliding down from the ridge, she moved like a shadow through the trees. Her mind already raced — if I cut the prisoner free, I'll have to fight the rest, but maybe the forest will answer me again…

Her heart pounded. She was alone, outnumbered, and weak from the wreck.

But her eyes gleamed with that same fire Lorenzo cursed her for.

Adventure had found her again.

Chapter 32: Strange Things

Nika crouched low, the saber gleaming faintly in her grip. She breathed in once, steadying herself. The villagers hadn't noticed her yet - too busy with their chanting, their fire, their prisoner.

"Alright, White Ghost," she whispered to herself. "One against twenty. Just another day."

She moved.

Her first strike was silent — a quick slice through the ropes that bound the prisoner. He fell like dead weight, gasping, but Nika caught him with one arm and whispered sharply:

"Quiet, or we both die."

Too late. One of the children shrieked. The scar-faced leader turned, his eyes catching the firelight, and roared a command. Spears lifted. Bows notched.

Nika grinned. "Good. I was getting bored."

…Wait a minute…Bored? Ha! You call fighting boring…

She kicked the fire, sending sparks exploding into the villagers' faces, and swung her saber in a wide arc. Two spears splintered in half. She twisted low, rolled through the dirt, and came up with her free hand raised.

"Mother Earth, lend me your hand," she hissed.

Roots ripped through the soil, snapping like whips, coiling around ankles and wrists. Several villagers crashed to the ground, shrieking in surprise. But more kept coming.

One spear flew straight for her head — she ducked, then hurled her saber like lightning. It struck the attacker's weapon, knocking it out of his grip. Another villager lunged with a club; Nika spun, grabbed the fallen spear, and cracked him across the jaw.

The air was thick with smoke, screams, and the roaring of the flames she had stirred into a frenzy. The forest answered her call - owls swooped down from the trees, screeching, tearing at faces with hooked talons.

Still, they came.

Scar-face himself charged, a massive ax in hand. Nika barely had time to brace — the blade slammed into the earth where she had stood a second before, shattering stone. She rolled, scooped up her saber again, and shouted:

"Spirits of the forest, bind him!"

The ground split open, vines exploding upward to wrap around Scar-face's arms and chest. He fought, roaring, ripping some apart with sheer strength. Nika lunged, slammed her boot into his chest, and sent him toppling backward into the flames. The fire roared high, swallowing his cry.

The rest broke. Terrified by the chaos - the fire, the birds, the roots that struck like snakes - they dropped their weapons and fled into the trees.

Silence fell, broken only by the crackling fire.

Nika staggered, panting, her strength fading. She pressed one hand to her knee, forcing herself upright. Then she looked down at the prisoner she had freed - bloodied, but alive, staring at her as though she were not human at all but something out of legend.

"Can you walk?" she asked.

He nodded weakly.

"Good," she said, hauling him to his feet. "Because we're not staying here."

She glanced once at the burning totems, then turned toward the forest. Her crew was waiting. And with them - questions more than answers.

By the time Nika dragged the half-conscious prisoner through the thickets, dawn was bleeding into the sky. Her clothes were torn, soot smeared across her face, and her saber hung loosely in her hand. Every step felt heavier than the last. But ahead, past the tangled brush, she saw it - smoke from a campfire, the faint sound of Santigo's laughter.

Home.

Or close enough.

She stepped out of the treeline, and three pairs of eyes locked on her at once.

"Mother of God!" Santigo yelped, jumping to his feet. "It's a ghost!"

"It's me, you fool," Nika rasped, then dropped the prisoner onto the sand with a dull thud.

Lorenzo's face darkened like a thundercloud. He stormed up to her, jaw tight, eyes blazing. "Are you out of your damned mind?"

"Nice to see you too," Nika muttered, wiping blood from her lip.

"You vanish in the middle of the day, nearly get yourself killed, come back at night dragging some half-dead lunatic out of the jungle, and you expect me to what? Clap my hands?" Lorenzo's voice rose with every word. "You'll get us all killed, witch!"

"Captain, enough," Taria cut in, though her eyes were full of worry as she looked Nika over. "She's bleeding."

"I've bled before," Nika said flatly, ignoring the sting in her side. "What matters is—" she jerked her chin toward the man on the sand—"this one was their prisoner. He may know something. Or he may not. Either way, I wasn't leaving him to die."

"Always playing the hero," Lorenzo spat. "One day you'll learn the world doesn't need saving by you alone."

Nika's eyes flashed. "And one day you'll learn that grumbling doesn't save lives."

For a heartbeat, the fire cracked between them, their glares like drawn swords. Then Santigo, always the fool, broke the tension by poking the prisoner with a stick.

"Uh... maybe we talk about the half-dead fellow before you two rip each other apart?" he said.

The man stirred, groaning. His eyes fluttered open — dark, filled with fear — and when they focused on Nika, he whispered a single word that made the hairs on her arms rise:

"Dragons..."

The fire sputtered in the silence that followed.

Nika crouched low, meeting his gaze. "What do you mean, dragons?"

But the man had already fallen back into unconsciousness.

Chapter 33: The Campfire

The campfire burned low, licking shadows across their tired faces. The prisoner sat apart, his wrists bound, his eyes wild from too many secrets. He leaned close to the flames and spoke in a low, fevered voice:

"I saw them... dragons. Their wings stretched wider than sails, their fire brighter than a hundred torches. The king of Italy... he seeks them. He will chain them, bend them to his crown. And when he does, no army in this world will stand against him. I saw them in Italy, or was it desert. But I saw them…"

His voice cracked, and silence fell heavy.

Lorenzo spat into the sand. "Dragons. Bah! Too much sun, too much sea, and now he babbles like a fool."

But Taria's face grew pale, her eyes locked on the firelight. "Nika," she whispered, "the book spoke of sand, of abyss, of sleep eternal. That is no sailor's tale. He may have seen something."

Nika's hand tightened around the book on her lap. She studied the prisoner carefully—his trembling, his madness, the way his story twisted. Then she stood, brushing sand from her clothes, and motioned her crew to follow her a little ways down the beach, away from the prisoner's ears.

Her voice was low, sharp as steel. "Listen to me. Dragons do not dwell in Italy. They live beneath the sands of the Sahara, in caves older than time. The book is clear. That fool speaks of seeing dragons in the desert and yet claims the Italian king hunts them here. His tale does not add up."

Santigo frowned. "So, he lies?"

"Or worse," Nika said, narrowing her eyes toward the prisoner. "He tells us half-truths. Maybe he saw something in the desert, maybe not. But mark me—

dragons are not in Italy. The king may search, but he will find nothing."

Taria's brow folded up. "Then what do we do?"

Nika's gaze turned out toward the black horizon where the sea whispered against the rocks. "We use him no longer. Tomorrow, Bubbles will carry us to Italy. There, we leave him. Let the king's men take back their traitor. We will take a ship south, to Africa, and seek the crystal where the sands swallow the sun."

Lorenzo nodded, though his jaw clenched. "For once, witch, I agree with you. Italy's as good a place as any to rid ourselves of dead weight."

They walked back to the fire. The prisoner looked up at them, hope flickering in his eyes, but Nika said nothing. She only fed another branch into the fire, watching the sparks leap upward like tiny dragons escaping into the night sky.

And in her heart, she whispered: If the king seeks fire, he will find only ash. But we... we know the truth.

Chapter 34: Departure to Italy

The night waned slowly, fire hissing into embers, the sea breathing heavy against the sand. Sleep was thin, restless, each of them turning over the prisoner's words in silence. By dawn, the sky bloomed pale gold, and gulls wheeled overhead.

Nika walked to the water's edge, her bare feet sinking into the cool surf. She raised her hands and called in the tongue of the sea. A deep tremor answered, rolling through the waves. Moments later, the water split as a massive shape rose from the depths—Bubbles, the great whale, his slick skin glowing in the morning light. He exhaled with a thunderous spray, then lowered his vast head toward Nika like an old friend.

"Bubbles," Nika whispered, stroking the curve of his eyebrow. "We need you again. Carry us far, across this sea. To Italy."

The whale moaned softly, as if in agreement, and drifted closer until his broad back brushed the shallows. One by one, the crew climbed aboard, gripping the ropes and harnesses Nika had tied long ago for such journeys. The prisoner was hauled last, tied firm so he could not slip away.

With a mighty sweep of his tail, Bubbles surged forward, the island shrinking behind them. Waves foamed white, and the horizon widened, endless blue. Hours passed, the sun rising high, the wind cooling their tired faces.

By evening, land appeared—hazy cliffs of stone, green hills rolling beyond them. Bells from a distant town rang faintly across the water.

"Italy," Taria breathed, her eyes bright with relief.

"Finally," Lorenzo muttered. "Civilization. Wine. Bread. A roof over our heads."

But Nika said nothing. Her gaze remained fixed on the prisoner, whose lips curved in a strange smile as the coast grew clearer. She did not trust him—not his tale of dragons, not his talk of kings.

"Tonight," she whispered to her friends so he could not hear, "we leave him here. He belongs to this land, not to our journey. Once he's gone, we'll find a ship south, and no one—not Charles, not kings, not prisoner—will stop us."

Bubbles carried them into a quiet cove, and they slipped into the shallows under cover of dusk. The crew leapt down into the surf, dragging the prisoner behind them. For a moment, the world felt still—their shadows long on the sand, the air heavy with salt and secrets.

Nika turned to her whale, pressing her palm against his skin. "Rest, old friend. Wait for me if you can. We will need you again."

Bubbles groaned low, then sank back into the sea, vanishing into the deep. The crew stood dripping on Italian soil, the prisoner bound between them, the scent of hearth smoke drifting from a village beyond the cliffs.

"Welcome to Italy," Nika said, her voice steady. "Now, let's find our ship to Africa."

And then, with a quick glance to her team, she raised her hand. In a flash of light, the four of them vanished from the quiet cove and reappeared on the bustling shore of Port Genoa, Italy—leaving the prisoner alone, bound and dumbfounded, staring at the empty sand where they once stood.

The port was alive with noise: fishermen shouting as they unloaded their catch, gulls circling for scraps, merchants calling out the prices of bread and olives. Between the masts of tall ships, the smell of tar and salt filled the air.

"There," Nika pointed, her eyes sharp. A sleek vessel rested at anchor, its polished hull catching the fire of the sunset. Painted across the stern was its name: Starlight.

"Perfect," Lorenzo muttered, licking his lips like a wolf who had spotted prey.

Slipping through the crowds, they moved like shadows. Taria whispered a small charm that dulled the sound of their steps, while Santigo distracted a drunken sailor with promises of dice games and cheap wine. Within moments, the crew was aboard.

Stealing the boat was easy. Keeping it—that was the hard part.

Chapter 35: The Curse of the Diamond

The Starlight cut through the waves of the Mediterranean, its sails swollen with warm winds driving them steadily south. Days blended into nights—salt on their lips, stars above their heads, and the endless sea beneath their feet. Nika stood at the bow, her white cloak billowing, eyes fixed on the horizon where Africa awaited.

One evening, after a simple dinner of roasted fish and flatbread stolen from the port, the crew gathered on deck around a lantern. The night was calm, the moon bright, and the waves whispered softly against the hull. Taria, seated cross-legged with her hair glowing faintly in the moonlight, looked at Nika.

"You asked why Zack wishes to be human again," she began softly. "I will tell you everything tonight. It is a long story, but you must listen carefully, because his fate is tied with ours."

Nika nodded, and the crew leaned closer. Even Lorenzo, usually grumbling, sat in silence with a furrowed brow.

"Once upon a time," Taria continued, "a king and a queen lived in a grand kingdom. The queen was wise and gentle, the kindest woman in the world. But the king…

he was harsh, greedy, always hungry for more gold. He commanded pirates to raid the seas, to plunder and fill his treasury. One day, the king learned of a sacred crystal hidden in the kingdom of dolphins—a diamond unlike any other, said to be 150,000 carats. It was not simply a jewel; it was life itself for the dolphins.

Each spring, under the full moon, the dolphins gathered in their sacred cave. The crystal absorbed the moon's energy and blessed their kind, so that their offspring were always born strong and healthy. Without it, their kingdom would vanish."

The crew listened intently. The sea was so quiet it seemed to hold its breath.

"The king ordered his pirates to steal it. They crept into the cave, tore the sacred diamond from its resting place, and brought it to the king. He hid it in his treasury, laughing, blind to the curse he had awakened. That very week, a son was born to the king and queen.

But far beneath the waves, the dolphins wept. Their leader, a great dolphin elder, was furious. He called upon the most ancient, forbidden magic. With it, he shed his form and became a man, walking upon the land. He came before the king with an ultimatum: return the diamond within twenty-four hours—or suffer. If the king refused, the dolphins would take his son and bind his fate to theirs."

Lorenzo whistled under his breath, but Taria's serious gaze silenced him.

"The king only laughed," Taria went on, her voice low and steady. "He mocked the elder and called him a charlatan, then ordered him cast out from the palace. The day passed. The king feasted, drank, and boasted of his riches. But when dawn came, the prince had vanished from his cradle. So had the diamond.

The king, desperate and trembling, went to the shore and fell to his knees. The elder dolphin rose from the waves and spoke: 'Your greed has cursed you. Your son is no longer yours. He belongs to the sea, to my people. He will live among us as a dolphin, never to return as a man unless fate itself allows it.'"

The lantern flickered, shadows dancing across their faces. Nika's fists tightened in her lap, her eyes narrowing with thought.

A hush fell over the deck. Even the ocean seemed to pause, listening.

Taria continued: ""How is this possible?" the king had cried on the shore, but the elder dolphin only shook his great head.

"You stole our diamond, but you did not know the truth," the elder said. "It is no mere gem. It is a sacred crystal, a living vessel of moonlight and sea. Through its power your child was born, marked by abilities no human possesses. That is why he cannot dwell among men." And with that, the elder turned and vanished beneath the waves, leaving the king broken.

The child, bound to the sea, took the form of a dolphin and grew among them. For twelve years he lived in the pod, swift and clever, beloved by the others. Yet when he came of age, the elder told him the truth: who he was, and what blood ran in his veins. The prince was given a choice—return to the human world, or remain with the dolphins.

He chose the sea. But from that day, a longing awoke in him. He began to watch the shores more often, to study ships, sailors, and kingdoms. Soon, he learned a sister had been born to the king and queen. From that moment, he swore an oath to protect her always, to follow her wherever she went, unseen but never absent."

Taria's voice softened into silence. The lantern cracked faintly, and the ocean groaned against the hull.

Nika blinked hard, as though trying to force the words to make sense. Finally, she whispered:

"You mean to tell me... Zack is my brother? My own blood... turned into a dolphin?"

"Yes." Taria's voice was gentle but firm.

Nika shaking to her feet, pacing the deck. "And you've been hiding this from me? All this time? How could you?"

Taria lowered her gaze. "Because I promised him. He feared it would break your heart, or burden you with questions you could not answer. He asked me to keep his secret."

Nika's fists clenched. "One thing I don't understand—if the dolphin elder had the spell to turn man into beast and beast into man, why can't Zack demand the same now? Why stay bound?"

Taria's eyes darkened. "Because the elder died nearly ten years ago. Only he knew the spell. The secret was buried with him."

For a long moment there was only the sound of the waves and the creak of the ropes. Then Nika drew in a slow, shaking breath, her face set with steel.

"Then I will find another way. I swear it—I will fulfill my brother's wish." She thought.

Her words hung heavy in the night air, as though even the stars had paused to listen.

That night, sleep would not come to Nika. She lay in her narrow hammock, staring at the timbers above her, her mind a storm. A thousand thoughts spun like restless winds: questions of fate, of family, of what it truly meant to be chosen. And always, one image returned—Zack, the dolphin who had never left her side, who now she knew was bound by blood.

Chapter 36: Shadows on the Hunt

Charles's team floated down the Amazon on a raft cobbled together from broken planks of their shattered ship. For days, the sun blistered their skin, and the river mocked them with endless bends. Hunger tormented, thirst clawed, and yet they pressed on—because hatred was stronger than pain.

Ios broke the silence first. "Captain, what's the plan when we reach Iota?"

Charles's voice was hoarse but steady. "We build. We steal. We sail again. The White Ghost will not outrun us."

But fate intervened before the island. By twilight of the fifth day, the river widened, and a fat-bellied merchant vessel drifted lazily nearby, its crew drunk on deck, lanterns swinging carelessly in the warm night air.

Alex's lips curled. "Why wait for Iota?"

They exchanged one look—and hunger turned to fury. Paddling hard, they lashed their raft to the ship and climbed aboard with blades in their teeth.

The fight was short, bloody. The drunken sailors screamed, but none survived the wrath of men who had already been half-dead on the river. By dawn, the merchant ship bore a new flag, its sails patched with stolen cloth, and Charles stood at the helm, breathing hard but victorious.

"This ship is ours," he spat into the wind. "Now—back to the hunt."

Below deck, Alex spread their half-burned map across a barrel. "Think. We don't even need this book. Nika's powers gave her the elements one by one: water, earth, fire, and air. The crystals follow the same order."

Ios leaned forward. "So, the next is fire. That means—dragons."

The word sank into the cabin like iron.

Lucas scowled. "Dragons in the desert… no ship, no crew, no sense. You're leading us straight into fire."

Charles slammed his fist on the map. "Better fire than shame. We are not shadows of that witch—we will take the crystal first, and when she comes, she'll find only smoke."

A silence fell, broken only by the groan of the stolen ship as it turned its bow toward the east. Toward Africa. Toward the Sahara.

Each man wondered privately if they were sailing toward glory… or into the jaws of death itself.

Nika's team approached Africa.

Chapter 37: Pearls of the Desert

"We nailed it!" Lorenzo said happily.

The team landed ashore, leaving their stolen ship moored at berth. The sun beat down on them mercilessly, the sand stretching in all directions like a golden ocean.

"Where are we?" Taria asked, shading her eyes.

"Perhaps Libya, perhaps Egypt... but wherever it is, it's where we need to be," Nika answered firmly.

Santigo squinted, sweat dripping from his brow. "And how exactly do we cross the Sahara? With our bare feet?"

"And where can we find a camel? They won't fall from the sky?!" Lorenzo barked, already languishing from the scorching heat. His boots were hot enough to fry an egg.

Nika paused, scanning the horizon. Suddenly, a faint mirage shimmered in the distance. No, not a mirage—a caravan, snaking slowly through the dunes. Camels with long necks, riders wrapped in flowing white robes.

"Do not hang up your nose, Captain—we are already there," Nika said with a grin and ran toward the caravan, her friends stumbling after her.

"Hey! Stop!" she shouted in Arabic as she neared. The riders pulled their camels to a halt, curious at the sight of such strangers.

"Where is this caravan going?" Nika asked.

"We are bound for Egypt, to Alexandria," one of the riders replied, his voice muffled under cloth.

"Could you sell us two camels?"

"Yes," the rider said, stroking his beast's neck, "but it will cost you five thousand dinars each."

"That's a huge amount!" Nika exclaimed.

"Our caravan," the man added with pride, "is the most expensive caravan in the world."

Nika turned back to her friends, frowning. "They want 5,000 dinars per camel. I don't have that kind of money."

"Negotiate," Santigo suggested, "you always talk your way through."

"Negotiation means I give something in return," Nika muttered. "And aside from this bag with crystals and the book, we have nothing to offer."

"Maybe we'll sell the fish," Lorenzo quipped, pointing at Taria with a sly grin.

"I'll sell you first," Nika snapped.

Lorenzo only laughed, finding joy in her temper.

Turning back to the caravan leader, Nika tried again. "Can we agree? I will give you my gold earrings and this copper medallion for two camels."

The Arab eyed the trinkets and shook his head. "For earrings and a medallion, I can give you one camel only."

Nika sighed. She looked at Taria. "Cry a little."

"But how?" Taria asked, puzzled.

"Look at the sun and don't blink for twenty seconds."

Taria obeyed, gazing into the blazing orb until her eyes watered. Soon, large tears rolled down her cheeks, shimmering as they fell. But instead of vanishing into the sand, each drop hardened into pearls—six of them, glowing like treasures from the sea.

Nika quickly gathered them into her palm and offered them. "Now... do we agree on two camels?"

The Arab's eyes widened. He had seen jewels, but never pearls born from tears. His smile betrayed his greed. "We agree."

Nika hugged Taria tightly. "Thank you, sister."

Meanwhile, Lorenzo and Santigo stood frozen, their mouths wide open.

"Shiver me timbers!" Lorenzo sputtered. "What in the devil's name was that?"

"Her tears," Nika said simply.

"Her...tears?" Santigo repeated, dumbfounded.

"Yes. When Atlanteans cry, their tears turn into pearls."

Santigo rubbed his chin, then muttered with a sly grin, "Captain, I'm beginning to think we should abandon this whole temple quest and just keep the princess with us."

"And I never cease to be amazed," Lorenzo said, still shaking his head, his eyes fixed on Nika as though waiting for her to reveal the next impossibility.

The camels were brought forward, tall, slow, and stubborn-looking. As Nika handed over the pearls, the caravan began to move again, leaving the four of them alone with their new beasts under the merciless sun.

Nika looked at her team, her expression steeled. "Now— let's see what secrets the Sahara has been hiding."

Chapter 38: The Oasis in the Dunes

"What are we waiting for? The temple won't find itself." Nika said, swinging onto her camel with a firm grip on the reins.

"She's right. It's time to go," Lorenzo grunted, pulling himself up with less grace but equal determination.

"Where exactly are we going?" Taria asked, already weary under the punishing sun.

"Follow the sandy abyss," Nika answered mysteriously, her eyes fixed on the horizon.

The caravan behind them disappeared into the shimmering distance as their small group pressed forward into the desert's emptiness. The heat bends the air into illusions—phantoms of water that vanished when approached. Their camels plodded silently, leaving deep prints in the golden sea.

Meanwhile, far away, Charles's stolen ship finally approached the northern shores of Africa. The crew, sunburnt and ragged, leaned against the railings.

"Alex," Lucas asked, squinting toward the endless horizon, "do you remember where the fire dragon tribe is? The place where the witch went five years ago?"

"I remember her talking about it," Alex replied, tightening his jaw. "If we sail southwest from Alexandria, then in six days we'll reach it."

"Yes..." Ios said, his voice trailing with nostalgia. "We got into such adventures with her, you can't even imagine. We saved the Indians from the conquistadors, prepared the wedding of the most beautiful princess in

India, even helped northerners build their houses and ships. And more... so much more."

His eyes softened as he stared at the waves. "We wouldn't have become pirates without her. Without her, we'd never have seen half the world."

Suddenly Alex spun around, his face burning with anger. He struck Ios across the cheek with a sharp slap.

"She is a witch who has no forgiveness!" Alex spat. "Don't you dare forget that. We will find the temple before her. Faster. And when we do, she'll pay."

Ios touched his stinging cheek, his gaze drifting towards the stern of the ship. The sea wind tugged at his hair, and a heavy sigh escaped his lips. And yet, he thought, this witch is a leader worth respecting—no matter what anyone says.

Back in the desert, Nika's team pressed on across the blazing sands. The sun was merciless, burning their skin, drying their lips.

"Maybe we can get some rest," Taria finally said, her voice thin. "My gills are shriveled without water. We've been walking for hours without pause. How will we survive this blistering heat?"

"The word of the princess is law," Lorenzo muttered, tugging at his collar, sweat pouring down his forehead.

"Fine then..." Nika pulled her camel to a halt. "We'll rest here. But don't forget—Charles is after us. We need to move fast."

They got down clumsily, exhaustion collapsing them into the sand. The heat radiating from the ground was unbearable. Soon, even in their weariness, Nika realized the truth: if they remained sprawled on the desert floor too long, sunstroke would claim them. Perhaps even death.

Closing her eyes, she clenched her fists and whispered to the earth. Calling on the last of her strength, she summoned the spirits of nature. The sand trembled, cracked, and from the barren land sprouted life.

A pool shimmered into existence, fed by a stream that bubbled from underground. Around it, palms unfolded their wide leaves, heavy with dates. Banana trees bent with fruit, and the ground softened with grass. A true oasis, born of desperation and magic.

Her vision blurred, and her body gave out. Nika stumbled to one of the palms, sank into the grass, and fell into a deep sleep.

Hours passed.

Taria was the first to wake up. Blinking against the sun, she caught sight of the water and gasped. Without hesitation she ran and dove straight into the pond, her laughter echoing across the dunes.

Lorenzo and Santigo awoke next, dragging themselves towards the sound. Their jaws dropped.

"Water!" Lorenzo shouted, then broke into a sprint. They plunged in after Taria, splashing like children, gulping down mouthfuls of the cool liquid.

"Where did this oasis come from?" Lorenzo cried joyfully.

"Or maybe we're still dreaming?" Santigo added, dunking his head beneath the water.

"Neither," Taria said, pointing at the palm where Nika lay sleeping peacefully. "It was Nika. She saved us again. Without her, we would have been dead long ago."

Lorenzo floated on his back, staring at the sky. "Now you won't surprise me with anything anymore."

He eventually waded ashore and began gathering dates, tossing a few into his mouth.

"Why would she use all her strength like this, if she has limits?" Santigo asked, shaking his head in wonder.

Taria's voice softened, full of quiet pride. "Because this is who she is. For the sake of the people close to her, she will do everything possible… and even the impossible."

They all glanced back at the sleeping Nika. For a moment, the desert seemed less harsh, the journey less impossible.

At that moment, Lorenzo realized that doubts and suspicions about Nika gradually dissipated, and he began to trust her more and more.

"What is actually in the temple?" he asked Taria.

"In the Temple," Taria replied, her voice hushed as if she were speaking of something sacred, "there are not only untold riches, but knowledge collected from all over the world in the form of books and manuscripts. There, you can find the answer to any question. The fate of a person is written there—don't ask me how, it's the secret of the temple. And most importantly... there, your greatest wish can be immediately fulfilled."

The words hung in the hot desert air. The pirates fell silent, lost each in thought.

Santigo smirked first. "Why would I need a wish if I can take as much gold as I want?" he thought greedily, picturing himself swimming in mountains of treasure.

Lorenzo's gaze shifted toward Nika, who still lay beneath the palm tree. His eyebrows furrowed. "Taria," he said quietly, "what does Nika want?"

Taria smirked mischievously. "Of course—the most gold. Can't you see?"

"That's a lie," Lorenzo snapped, narrowing his eyes.

"Of course, it's a lie." Taria's tone softened, almost protective.

"Then tell me honestly," Lorenzo pressed, "what does she really want?"

Taria hesitated, her lips parting but no words coming out at first. Finally, she sighed. "To be honest... I'm not entirely sure."

A heavy pause settled over them. The desert wind carried grains of sand across their camp, whispering like secrets.

Then, from the shade, Nika's voice cut through. "You will find out about my desire," she said calmly, her eyes opening, "but you'll have to wait a little bit."

The camp fell silent. Even the camels shifted uneasily, as if they, too, felt the weight of her words.

Nika sat up, brushing the sand from her arms. "We still have about two days' to travel. Maybe less."

"Do you know where it is?" Santigo asked skeptically.

"Yes and no..." Nika replied, her lips curving into a sly smile.

134

"How is it 'yes and no'?" Santigo wouldn't let it go.

"You'll see for yourself," Nika answered, her tone mysterious.

Here Lorenzo broke into the conversation. "Tell me, how long ago did you get fire abilities?"

Nika's gaze lingered on the flames of their small campfire, her face illuminated by its glow. "Not long ago," she admitted, her voice low, almost reverent. "Fire was the hardest to master. Water and earth—those came naturally, like breathing. But fire..." She paused, a flicker of memory flashing across her eyes. "Fire burns you if you don't respect it. To summon it, I had to face it. Not just outside, but inside myself. My anger. My fear. My weakness. That was the price."

The group listened quietly, for once without jokes or complaints.

Chapter 39: The Gift of Fire

The desert night wrapped itself around the camp. The fire crackled and spat, glowing red and gold against the endless black dunes. Everyone leaned forward—Santigo with his arms crossed but eyes betraying curiosity, Lorenzo chewing a date but not tasting it, and Taria resting her chin on her knees, knowing more than the others. And then Nika began to speak.

"It happened a couple of years ago, in Alexandria," she said slowly, letting the words carry the weight. "The library there—its shelves are endless, scrolls and manuscripts piled high like mountains. I spent weeks lost in its corridors, reading everything I could find: sea maps, forgotten myths, magical studies. And then, one evening, I stumbled on a manuscript unlike any other. It smelled of age, its ink almost faded, but its words burned in me. It spoke of the Sahara—but not as we know it. Long ago, that land was not desert. It was called Dracardia."

The name hung in the air.

"In Dracardia lived dragons," Nika continued. "Not monsters, not beasts of nightmares, but a tribe—wise, noble, and strong. They lived among humans, spoke our language, shared our bread and fire. They gave warmth to villages, carried burdens with their wings, healed wounds with their flames. They were protectors and companions, and the people loved them. For centuries it was so. But as always, word spread. And greed listens better than gratitude."

She glanced at Santigo. "The northern tribes heard of these creatures and grew jealous. They saw not friends, but weapons. Dragons meant fire without end, wings for war, strength for labor. So they marched against Dracardia."

Her voice is hardened. "The war lasted years. It was brutal, merciless. Rivers ran red. Hatred poisoned hearts. And the dragons, who had only ever wanted peace, were forced to kill those they once called friends. Yet still they stayed beside their people. But something began to change. Dragons can see what men cannot. They see the aura—the light around a soul. And where once that light had been bright, it darkened. Black crept into it, until whole armies glowed with nothing but shadows. The dragons saw this and knew: mankind was losing itself."

The fire snapped, throwing sparks into the night.

"The last dragons, desperate, made a choice. They gathered in a ring around the armies, encircling them. In the center stood the mightiest of them all, the Red One, older than mountains. He drew in breath and roared—a roar that split the heavens. From his mouth burst fire, but not ordinary fire. It was molten earth itself, lava pouring across the land, devouring trees, stone, life. The flames spread, faster than wind, until the battlefield was drowned. But even then—" Nika's voice softened, "—they did not kill the humans. The flames touched them, and instead of burning, they turned into sand. In an instant, became thousands of grains scattered on the wind."

A heavy silence fell.

"The ring of dragons, one by one, sank into the ground, sealing themselves away. And the Red One at the center... sacrificed himself. His body turned into a vast eye, carved into the desert floor. It still stars upward, forever open. The Eye of the Dragon. And thus Dracardia died, and the Sahara was born."

Lorenzo muttered a curse under his breath.

"But the dragons left behind a spell," Nika continued, her eyes glamping with memory. "A promise. That one day, if a pure soul found the Eye and pulled free the black spear thrust into its heart, the spell would break. The people of sand would rise and live again. And the dragon, too, would return."

Her companions leaned closer, the firelight flickering on their faces.

"When I read this, I couldn't stop thinking about it. I had to see it with my own eyes. I crossed the desert, step by step, days into weeks. And then—I found it. A great, endless circle of stone, and in the center, a massive eye carved into the earth, larger than a ship. And there, lodged deep, was the black spear."

She paused, staring into the flames. "I grabbed it. Pulled with all my strength. Again and again. But it would not budge. I circled the Eye, wondering what I was doing wrong. And then... it hit me. Pain. Terrible pain. Not mine, but his. The dragon's pain, centuries old, poured into me. It burned my chest, my veins, my soul. I fell to my knees, tears scorching my cheeks. And in that agony I whispered: 'I will help you.' And then—like it had been waiting only for those words—the spear slide free."

The fire flared high, as though echoing her words.

"The earth groaned. The sands split beneath me, and I fell. Darkness swallowed me whole. When I woke, I was in a cavern vast beyond imagination, its walls glittering with veins of fire. And around me... dragons. Dozens. Their scales shimmered like jewels, their eyes glowed like suns. They lowered their heads. And then, from among them, a great red dragon emerged. His scales were scarlet flame, his wings blotting out the cavern light. He came to me, and without opening his mouth, spoke in my mind: 'My name is Nino. You freed me. Only a heart pure enough to feel my pain could break the curse. You did.'"

Nika's hand trembled, but her voice did not falter. "I asked him about the people—the ones who had become sand. He said: 'When the first rain falls upon the desert, they will return to flesh, and the Sahara will bloom into a garden again.' And then he looked at me, and his voice rumbled like thunder: 'You restored our faith in mankind. You deserve a gift.'"

Her eyes blazed. "Then it happened. A great bubble, clear as glass, formed around me. Nino opened his jaws, and fire—pure, endless fire—flooded into it. Flames licked, coiled, wrapped around me. Yet I felt no pain. Only warmth. I spun inside the bubble, fire flowing through me, into me, until it burst from my palms like rivers of light. When the bubble sank to the ground and vanished, I stood changed. Fire was mine. And Nino's voice filled me one last time: 'Now you carry the magic of fire. Use it well.'"

Nika fell silent. The desert wind sighed.

Chapter 40: The Mountain Cave

Unbelievable," muttered Santigo, rubbing the back of his neck, still struggling to take in Nika's tale. Dragons, deserts, ancient curses—his world of sails and cannons felt suddenly small.

"Of course," Nika said with a faint smile, "after that we became friends. And I have visited Nino more than once."

The words hung in the dry desert air like sparks before a storm.

That evening they made camp under the open sky. The stars burned sharp and cold, countless and watchful. The fire they kindled gave little warmth against the chill, and yet everyone was too tired to complain. Slowly, one by one, they drifted into sleep—Santigo still muttering something about "fire-breathing lizards," Lorenzo lying awake longer than the rest, his doubts fighting with the trust Nika had begun to earn.

At dawn, the desert turned gold. The travelers rose, ate dates in silence, mounted their camels, and set off again. The desert stretched endlessly, sand shifting like waves, until last a dark shadow rose from the horizon.

They travelled couple hours and then…a miracle…

"Oh, that's the same mountain!" Nika exclaimed, her eyes brightening.

"Have we arrived?" Taria asked, shading her eyes with her hand.

"Not quite." Nika pointed. "We need to go around it. There's a secret door."

The camels plodded on, carrying them along the mountain's edge. The closer they drew, the larger it loomed, jagged and ancient, as if it had risen straight out of the earth in defiance of time itself.

At last Nika stopped. She slide down from her camel and placed her palm against the stone wall. "Here," she whispered.

The team followed, exchanging uneasy glances. Their path ended at a colossal disk of stone fitted seamlessly into the mountain. No seams, no handles, only a flat face carved with spirals faintly glowing in the shade.

"What's next?" Lorenzo asked, frowning. "We knock?"

Nika stepped before the stone, raised her hands, and closed her eyes. Her lips moved, shaping syllables strange and thick:

"*Goga boga dari bas ica bica vini vas!*"

The words echoed off the mountain, deep and otherworldly. The air trembled, dust rained down, and slowly—groaning like a living thing—the stone disk began to turn. A sliver of darkness opened, then widened into a towering doorway. Cool air, tinged with the faint scent of ash and embers, rushed out.

The others stared in silence.

"Nino taught me this spell," Nika said, lowering her hands, "so that I could visit him whenever I needed."

They stepped into the mountain. The cavern was vast, walls glimmering with veins of firestone, their glow pulsing like the breath of something alive. Yet they had no time to marvel. From the shadows, huge figures emerged—dragons, bronze and silver, their eyes blazing like twin suns.

The guards had found them.

Before anyone could move, the dragons closed ranks, wings half-spread, spears of flame gathering in their throats. The air grew so hot it stung the skin.

"Down! Weapons down!" Lorenzo barked, instinct pulling him to protect his crew, but it made no difference. The guards surged forward, herding them with terrifying precision.

Within minutes, they were led into a great chamber—the throne hall. The roof soared like the heavens themselves, its arches formed by stalactites glowing faintly red. And upon a throne of black stone, coiled and resplendent, sat a dragon greater than the rest.

Nino!

His scales shimmered crimson like living fire, his horns curved like molten iron. But when his eyes fell upon Nika, they softened, glowing with recognition.

"Who do I see!" His voice thundered not from his mouth but inside their very heads. "My dear Nika—has fate brought you back to me? After so long?"

He reared slightly, and then his massive jaws spread into what could only be called a smile. "Everybody, it's Nika! Guards, let them go! These are my best guests!"

The guards instantly lowered their heads and withdrew. The suffocating heat faded, replaced by a warmth that felt almost like welcome.

Nika stepped forward, her hand pressed to her chest in greeting. "Nino, I am glad to see you too. But yes—you are right. I've come back not for leisure, but for business. I need to speak with you. Alone."

The great dragon's head lowered. "Come."

He led her through an archway into a side cavern, a chamber vast but strangely intimate, lit with pools of glowing fire. There were no treasures here, only stone, and the smell of earth and smoke.

"I am listening," said Nino, settling onto the ground, his scarred wings folding like a cloak.

Nika took a breath. She reached into her bag, pulled out the book and the crystals, and laid them before him. Their glow filled the chamber.

"The Temple of the Seven Seas exists," she said simply.

Nino's eyes widened. His entire body shifted, scales scraping stone. "Impossible! That cannot be. I thought it was only a myth."

"Then look," she said, sliding the book towards him.

The dragon bent low, enormous claws careful as he turned page after page. His talons traced the symbols, his great head moving closer, disbelief, looking and reading every line. "It cannot be... and yet here it is... written plain before me."

He looked up. "Nika, tell me everything."

So she did. She told him of the journey—the book's appearance, the crystals they had found, the battles with Charles, the betrayals, the storm, the island, and the path that had finally led them back to him. She spared no detail.

Nino listened, his golden eyes never leaving her face. When she finished, he rumbled low in his chest, a sound like distant thunder.

"I will stand beside you," he said at last. "Whatever happens, whatever comes, you will not face it alone. My fire is yours." His lower headed close enough that his hot breath stirred her hair. "But know this, Nika: I have lived here for centuries, my tribe has scoured every dune, every cavern, and yet... never once have we found such a crystal. If it exists, it lies hidden even from us."

She was disappointed, opening the book, leafing through its pages again, her eyes narrowing at every line, but no clue revealed itself.

Frustration burned at her chest. She snapped the book shut and turned back toward the others waiting outside.

Her friends looked up eagerly.

Chapter 41: The Temple of Fire

"Well, my team," Nika said at last, her voice echoing faintly in the dragon's cavern, "the book doesn't say exactly where to look for the crystal."

Lorenzo crossed his arms, already restless. "And what do we do now, White Ghost? Walk circles in the sand until we collapse?"

Nika's eyes narrowed in thought. She turned toward the firelit walls. "No. If the book led us to the kingdom of dragons, then the crystal is here. It has to be. Dragons are fire's guardians—and if there is any place to search for the fire crystal, this is it."

Before anyone could answer, Nika spread her feet apart, inhaled deeply, and raised her arms. "It's time to call on the fire itself."

Her friends exchanged uncertain glances. Even Nino tilted his massive head, smoke curling from his nostrils.

Nika closed her eyes and began to dance. Slowly at first—measured steps, her arms flowing in a ritual as old as the sands. Her lips murmured words none of them had heard before.

"The Makindzi," whispered Taria in awe.

Her body swayed, circling, stamping, leaping. The air shimmered with heat. Then sparks burst from her fingertips, blazing into fireballs of different sizes. They floated out from her palms and began to orbit around her, faster and faster, until the chamber glowed red with their furious dance.

Lorenzo stopped breathing. Santigo muttered a prayer. Taria clasped her hands together, eyes wide. Even Nino, a dragon born of fire, lowered his head with reverence.

The flames whirled tighter, forming spirals and knots in the air, like fiery constellations. Then suddenly they froze, clustered together, and stretched into a vast, living screen of fire that hung before Nika like a burning mirror.

Its center flared, blinding white, and an image began to appear.

Nika's eyes snapped open. She saw it—clear as if she stood there already. A temple of clay and stone, vast and tiered like a ziggurat, its surface carved with spirals and ancient runes. A river of molten lava wound before its gates. And barring the way—an impossible waterfall of sand, forever pouring down to block the entrance.

She gasped, breaking the dance. The fireballs hissed out one by one, leaving only smoke and silence. Without a word, she turned and sprinted out of the cavern.

"Nika!" Lorenzo barked, stumbling after her. Santigo swore and followed. Taria gathered her skirts and ran too.

They stopped only when Nika froze, breathless, pointing to the distance.

And there it was.

The temple inside a cave. Just as she had seen.

It rose from the earth like a mountain carved by gods, its sides terraced, decorated with strange ornaments and twisting forms. Above its gate the sand-waterfall poured endlessly, glowing faintly in the sun, while the river of lava hissed and cracked below, filling the air with burning fumes.

All this time, Nino had been silently following. His enormous wings folded against his sides, his eyes blazing as he looked upon the place.

"Nino," Nika said, turning to him, "can you read that description above the waterfall?"

The dragon narrowed his eyes. "Yes," he rumbled. "This is the language of the Creators."

The chamber fell silent as Nino shut his eyes. He began to speak. No-grow. No-chant. The sounds were layered, otherworldly. Sometimes a rumble so deep the ground quaked, sometimes a high-pitched wail that pierced their ears. His voice rolled like thunder and howled like storms, a tongue that no human tongue could hold.

Minutes passed. Sweat dripped down Santigo's face. Lorenzo pressed his palms to his ears. Taria whispered a prayer to the old gods.

And then—Nino roared.

The sound shook the entire mountain. A shockwave blasted outward, knocking the team to the ground. Stones cracked. Dust filled the air.

When it cleared, the waterfall of lava had stopped. The cascade froze mid-air, then dissolved into dust, revealing at last the black stone doors of the temple.

"Quickly! Get on me!" Nino growled, lowering his massive body.

The team scrambled onto his back, gripping his scales. Nino spread his colossal wings, leapt forward, and soared over the lava river in one sweep. The heat seared their faces, but they clung tight until the dragon landed before the gate.

With a massive roar, Nino unleashed a torrent of flame. It struck the bronze bowl that sat in the temple's center.

Instantly, the bowl erupted in brilliant fire, light flooding the temple hall until it gleamed like molten gold.

They stepped down, staring in awe.

"Where is the crystal?" Nika said aloud, her voice echoing through the chamber. "Let's spread out—search everywhere!"

The team split. Lorenzo and Santigo hurried down a side hall lined with carvings of winged serpents. Taria wandered beneath a vast dome, tracing inscriptions with her fingers.

Nino rose into the air, circling above them. From up high, he could see more. He scanned the walls, the floor, every corner—until his golden eyes caught a glimmer.

A figurine. Small, delicate, shaped like a dragon, its body shimmering faintly as if alive.

He swooped lower. The figurine rose into the air of its own accord, glowing brighter with each second.

As he reached for it, the glow burst into flame. It blazed in his paw, searing bright—and Nino's heart leapt.

"This is it!" he roared. His voice shook the temple. "Hurry! Come to me—I found it!"

But the moment he spoke, the temple shuddered. A deep groan rolled through the walls. Cracks split the pillars. Sand poured down like rain.

"Move!" Nika screamed.

Stones collapsed, crushing the floor where they had stood only seconds before. The river of lava surged louder, as if the temple itself was dying.

Nino dove, his wings sweeping debris aside. He scooped the team into his massive claws and soared towards the exit. Boulders fell around them, flames licked the walls, sand poured like an avalanche.

The dragon's wings beat furiously, dodging, weaving, until with one final surge he burst through the gates. Behind them, the temple groaned, split, and collapsed entirely, swallowed by sand and fire.

On the far side of the lava river, Nino landed, chest heaving. He opened his paw, and there—gleaming like captured flame—rested the fire crystal.

He lowered his head, his eyes solemn. "Use it for good."

Nika cupped the crystal, its warmth searing into her palms. She nodded. "I will."

Beside her, Lorenzo slide to the ground, trembling with exhaustion. "Finally out..." he muttered, wiping his brow.

"Well?" Santigo gasped, half-laughing, half-shaking. "I almost wet my pants in there, Captain."

Taria pressed her hands together, her face pale but steady. Nika stood taller, the crystal burning in her hands, and for a moment they all stared at it in silence— knowing that nothing would ever be the same again.

"After all these crazy adventures," Lorenzo said at last, dragging his boots through the sand, "I need to rest. And drink. A lot."

Alright then, we can organize it!" the dragon king exclaimed with boyish joy, rubbing his mighty paws together. His booming laughter echoed through the cavern halls, bouncing against the high ceilings like thunder.

"Nino, we can't—" Nika began, but her words were cut short.

"Of course, Your Majesty," Lorenzo interrupted smoothly, bowing with a theatrical sweep. "We can stay one more day and have fun. Who in their right mind would deny a dragon's invitation?"

Nino's eyes glimmered with firelight, his long teeth flashing in a grin. "I will give the order to prepare for feasting and joy!"

Nika shot a sharp glance at Lorenzo. As the dragon turned away to bark orders in their guttural tongue, she leaned closer and whispered fiercely, "You know we cannot stay, we need to hurry. Every wasted hour brings us closer to danger."

Lorenzo shrugged, hands behind his back, smug as always. "First of all, no one is chasing us. Second, the temple isn't going to sprout legs and walk away, nor will the crystals vanish. We deserve one night, White Ghost. One night of rest."

Nika opened her mouth to retort, but hesitation flickered across her face. Her shoulders dropped. "...Perhaps you are right," she said softly, surprising even herself.

Within the hour, the dragons had prepared everything: banquet tables stretched like rivers through the cavern halls, torches crackled along the walls, and dishes filled with roasted meats, fire-fruits, and bowls of glowing embers that dragons ate as delicacies.

Nika, exhausted from the fire ritual and the temple ordeal, allowed herself to be guided to the guest

149

chambers. She dropped her bag with a dull thud, collapsed on the stone bed covered in silk cushions, and fell into sleep almost instantly.

Meanwhile, her companions were swept up into the feast. Dragons toasted them with cups carved from gemstones, the air filled with roaring songs and fiery displays of magic. Taria was charmed by the musicians—dragons plucking strings of flame. Santigo and Lorenzo ate until their belts strained, each giving the other to try stranger dishes. For a while, laughter filled the cavern, and the world's dangers felt impossibly far away.

But Lorenzo's mind was elsewhere.

In the middle of a drinking contest with Santigo, he suddenly remembered her. Nika.

Leaving the firelit halls behind, he walked quietly through the corridors, the echoes of dragon laughter fading into silence. He found her door half open, and stepped inside.

There she was.

Sleeping peacefully, her face softened without the weight of command or danger. For a moment he simply stood there, watching her. He remembered how, when they first met, he had thought she was unbearable—a reckless witch with too much pride. But now... Now he saw her courage, her self-sacrifice, her endless kindness. He saw how she carried her team as if their lives were her own.

And something inside him shifted.

A burning desire rose in him, so strong it started even Lorenzo, the man who feared nothing. He wanted to lean down, to kiss her, to confess without words what had been growing in his chest.

His lips hovered inches away.

But he stopped.

Gritting his teeth, he straightened, pulling the blanket higher over her shoulders instead. With a sigh that sounded almost like defeat, he turned and slipped out, leaving her undisturbed.

Part VI: Fairies and The Unknown

Chapter 42: He Is Back

Hours passed. The great feast dwindled, torches dimmed, songs died down. One by one, dragons and humans alike fell into the deep sleep, lying across banquet tables and stone floors.

Silence claimed the mountain.

Except...

Far below, at the foot of the desert mountain, Charles's ship finally touched land.

The men dragged their weary bodies across the sand, their eyes glowing with the hunger of revenge.

"Doesn't it seem strange to you," Lucas whispered, staring up at the dark silhouette against the starry sky, "that in the middle of this endless desert, a mountain rises like a giant's tooth?"

"There must be an entrance," Alex replied coolly. "We need to go around."

"And then what?" Lucas pressed, impatient, sweat dripping from his temple.

They circled the base until at last Alex's eyes widened. He pointed. "There. The disk. Just like she said."

His fingers brushed the ancient stone circle, cold under his palm. Taking a deep breath, he spoke the words of power—the same incantation Nika had once taught him, never imagining he'd use it against her.

The stone rumbled. Grinding, groaning, it rolled aside, revealing the black maw of the dragon cave.

Charles's lips curled into a grin. "Finally."

Inside, the mountain slumbered. Guards leaned against their spears, heads drooped, their chests rising in the deep sleep of overindulgence. The air still smelled of roasted meat and firefruit wine.

It was child's play for Charles and his men to slip past the guards.

Like shadows, they entered the very heart of the dragon king's domain.

"Where could she be?" Ios whispered, his voice barely audible in the echoing cavern.

"Oh, I know. In the palace of the king—she mentioned him," Lucas muttered.

Charles's eyes are narrowed. "Then we split up. The faster we search, the faster we find her. No mistakes."

The men scattered like shadows across the sleeping dragon city.

It was Ios who found her first.

The chamber door creaked ever so slightly as he pushed it open, his heart hammering in his chest. Torchlight from the hallway flickered across the room. There, in the far corner, was a bag. His eyes widened—he recognized it instantly. The book. The crystals. Everything Charles desired.

And there, asleep on the bed, was Nika.

Ios moved silently across the floor, step by careful step. He bent, lifted the bag, and then hesitated. His hand trembled as he reached out and lightly touched Nika's shoulder.

"Wake up, Nika," he whispered urgently. "Wake up."

Her eyes snapped open, clear as ice. In an instant, her palm flashed with magic, shaping into a jagged icicle dagger that pressed against his throat. The chill bit into his skin, drawing a thin line of frost.

"Don't make noise," Ios breathed, raising a finger to his lips. "Please... let me speak."

Her gaze was sharp, unyielding. "Speak then. But know I can end you with one movement."

Ios dropped to his knees, desperation in his eyes. "Forgive me. Forgive us—for betraying you, for falling into Charles's service. You were right! Always right! Alex twisted my mind, cornered me. I didn't have a choice... but I can choose now. I want to return to you, to your team—if you'll have me. If not... then I won't go back to Charles either."

Nika's dagger did not waver. Her eyes pierced through him, searching for the smallest flicker of deception. "And what guarantee do I have you won't betray me again?"

153

Without a word, Ios lifted the bag he had taken. He placed it gently at her feet. "This," he said firmly. "I could've slipped away with your book and crystals. I could've slit your throat while you slept. But I didn't."

The dagger melted in Nika's hand. She leaned back, still watching him carefully. "...You've got a point. So, what's your plan?"

"We move now, before Charles realizes. Wake your team, slip away in the dark. By the time he notices my absence, we'll be long gone. We gain time, Nika. That's the only way to win."

Nika studied him for a moment longer, then gave a single nod. "Fine. But know this—if I even suspect you of signaling Charles, I'll kill you without hesitation."

Ios swallowed and nodded. "Understood."

She picked up the bag and smirked. "And we'll leave the book. I've already learned all I needed. Let Charles puzzle out the riddles—it'll keep him busy." She turned toward the door. "We're heading to Tibet."

Ios blinked. "For the last crystal?"

"Yes. High in the mountains...among the clouds of the fairies."

Moments later, Nika woke the others.

Santigo grumbled, rubbing his eyes. Lorenzo muttered curses under his breath as he buckled his belt. "What's the rush? And what is he doing here?"

Nika sighed and told them briefly of Ios's visit, of Charles's nearness.

Lorenzo's eyes went wide. "You be jokin' with me?"

She smiled, shaking her head. "No joke, Captain. And no other choice."

Meanwhile, Charles stormed into the same chamber only an hour later. His eyes fell on the bed, the bag... and the empty space where the crystals should have been. He snatched up the book, flipping through its pages. His jaw clenched.

"Ios..." he grew, the word dripping with venom. "He's betrayed us." Slamming the book shut, Charles barked: "We're leaving. Now."

His men followed him back out of the dragon's halls, their shadows swallowed by the night.

By dawn, Nika's team reached the familiar oasis. The cool water shimmered under the morning sun, and weary as they were, they felt relief wash over them.

Taria wasted no time—she leapt into the pool with a graceful splash. Santigo knelt to light a fire, striking sparks until the flames crackled to life. Lorenzo and Ios scrambled up palm trees, tossing down clusters of sweet dates.

Meanwhile, Nika moved slowly around the camp, her hands glowing faintly as she zapped beetles, snakes, and scorpions with flicks of magic. Her eyes never stopped scanning the horizon.

Refreshed, Taria emerged from the pool and settled by the fire, her hair dripping. "I have a wonderful idea," Nika said suddenly, sitting cross-legged on the sand. "A way to shorten our path."

"Oh?" Lorenzo raised a brow. "And how's that?"

"We head to Egypt. Hurghada. There we board a ship, sail down the Red Sea into Arabia. From there, we follow the Bay of Bengal into India. Once in India, we take elephants through the mountains to Nepal, then across the Himalayas into the realm of the fairies."

The group sat stunned at her confidence.

"That's madness," Santigo muttered.

"Madness or not, it'll take months," Lorenzo added grimly. "A month on water, another across land. It's too long." He smirked and leaned back on his elbows. "How about... an even shorter way?"

Chapter 43: The Leap to Egypt

"Let me think..." Nika said, her brow furrowing as the firelight flickered across her face. "Since I have teleportation, I can only move for short distances, and only to those places where I've already been. Accordingly... I could try to move us to Egypt. There, from Hurghada, I'll call Bubbles. On his back, we can ride through the seas all the way to India. It should take no more than three days, and once there, perhaps we can get elephants to reach the mountains."

"Wait, Nika," Taria said, glancing at her with concern. "Can you really move us that far? Isn't it too dangerous?"

Nika hesitated for a moment, then nodded. "It is far... very far. And yes, it will exhaust me, maybe even leave me unconscious for a time. But we don't have the luxury

156

of waiting. If we don't try, Charles will always be on our trail. So I'll do it, no matter the cost."

The fire crackled between them. Lorenzo leaned back on his hands, his face half in shadow. "Very well then. We'll do it tomorrow." His lips curled into a sly smile. "Tonight, we eat."

"And what do we have for dinner?" Taria asked hopefully, glancing around.

Nika grinned mischievously. "Fried beetles, roasted scorpions... or dates. Your choice."

The two men grimaced at once, wrinkling their noses as though she'd set a rotten fish in front of them.

"No thanks," Santigo said flatly, waving his hand. "We're not hungry."

"Suit yourselves," Nika said with a shrug. She popped a roasted beetle into her mouth, crunching it with exaggerated enjoyment. "But remember, this journey will take every ounce of our strength. Dates alone won't carry you far. You need protein—even if it crawls."

Ios reached for a beetle without hesitation and bit into it with a loud crunch. "She's right. They're actually tasty."

Lorenzo lifted an eyebrow, watching Ios chew. He sighed, reached for one, and held it over the fire briefly. Slowly, dramatically, he puts it into his mouth. "Although, you know, Santigo... we've eaten worse. Rotten biscuits, half-spoiled fish, even rat stew once in Havana. Can't we stomach a little bug?"

"As you say, Captain," Santigo muttered darkly. Still, grimacing as though he were facing execution, he grabbed a scarab, closed his eyes, and forced it down.

157

Taria watched them both, disgust and amusement fighting on her face. At last, she plucked one beetle, took a deep breath, and popped it in. She chewed quickly, swallowed, and shuddered. But then—curiously—her face softened. "It's not... as terrible as I thought."

Soon, one after another, the beetles disappeared into hungry mouths, and the campfire flickered with laughter. What had begun with grimaces ended with chuckles, and by the end, even Santigo was licking his fingers.

Morning dawned bright and merciless over the desert. The team woke up groggy but determined. Nika stood, brushing the sand from her pirate clothes, her expression was serious.

Lorenzo approached her, adjusting his coat. "Are you ready?"

"More than ever," she replied firmly. Then she glanced back at their resting animals. "What about the camels?"

"Leave them here," Ios said with a shrug. "They'll find their own way. They're creatures of the desert."

But Nika shook her head. She walked to the camels and gently removed their reins. Placing her hand on their soft muzzles, she whispered, "Now you are free. Go where you wish."

The camels blinked, then to everyone's shock, one spoke in a low, surprised voice: "You... you understand us?"

The others froze, staring in disbelief.

"Yes," Nika said softly, stroking her neck. "And I tell you—you are free. You are no longer bound. The desert is yours again."

The camels bowed their heads in gratitude. "We thank you, White Ghost," they said in unison before running gracefully into the dunes, their shapes swallowed by the endless waves of sand.

The team exchanged bewildered glances.

"Every day with her is something new," Santigo muttered.

"Come," Nika said, stepping back towards them. "Take each other's' hands. Hold tightly, and don't let go."

They formed a circle, gripping each other's hands. The air around Nika shimmered, heat waves rising from her body. The sand began to tremble beneath their feet. A deep hum filled the air as she chanted words older than memory.

Suddenly, the world lurched. Light blinded them. The earth groaned and cracked. And in a flash—everything twisted, bent, and tore apart.

When the light faded, they were standing on cobblestones. The scent of salt filled their lungs. The sound of gulls echoed overhead.

They had arrived in Hurghada, Egypt.

But Nika lay collapsed on the stones, her chest rising and falling weakly. Lorenzo immediately scooped her into his arms, holding her close.

"She… she truly did it," Taria whispered, awe in her voice.

"She's a hero," Ios said solemnly, his eyes fixed on Nika's pale face.

"Yes, but she needs rest," Taria added, her brow furrowed. "I will summon Bubbles. He will carry us swiftly."

"Not so fast," Lorenzo said sharply. "Don't call that sea beast yet. Maybe we can find a ship. Sail like normal people."

Ios crossed his arms. "Your 'wooden toy' will take weeks. That creature will take us in days."

Lorenzo hesitated, his jaw tightening. At last, with a groan, he muttered: "I cannot believe I'm saying this... but fine. Call Bubbles."

Chapter 44: Road to the Fairies

Taria dove into the sea, her silver hair fanning out in the water like threads of moonlight. She let out a long, powerful ultrasound call, her voice traveling far through the deep. The ocean answered. In less than ten minutes, the water trembled as a colossal shadow rose from the abyss. A mighty blue whale breached the waves—Bubbles, their old and loyal friend.

With a soft groan that made the sea itself shiver, the whale floated near the shore. Lorenzo carefully lifted Nika into his arms, carrying her like something fragile. One by one, the team clambered up the slippery sides and slipped inside through the whale's enormous mouth.

The next few days... were the most disgusting ride of their lives.

The air was humid, heavy with the stink of seawater and fish. The walls pulsed faintly, and the entire chamber rocked as if the world itself was tossing them around. Storms raged outside, great waves hammering Bubbles, but inside, they were safe—safe, though nauseated, sliding across slimy flesh whenever the whale dove or twisted.

…Yikes...

"Never. Ever. Ever… again," Santigo murmured, holding his stomach. "If we live through this, I'll kiss the ground and swear loyalty to dry land forever."

Lorenzo just rolled his eyes. "You complain too much. It's better than sinking."

Taria ignored them, sitting near Nika, who had not yet stirred. For three days, she watched over her captain, whispering to her, checking her breathing, waiting for the moment her eyes would open again.

And then, finally, they did.

Nika blinked slowly, her vision adjusting to the dim, wet chamber around her. She lifted her head weakly. "Did... did everything work out? Are we... inside Bubbles?"

"You finally woke up!" Taria exclaimed, hugging her tightly, relief bursting in her voice. "You slept for three days! I thought you'd never wake, I was so worried."

"Good morning," Lorenzo said dryly from the other side, though the faint smile at the corner of his mouth betrayed his relief. "How did you sleep, Sleeping Beauty?"

"Fine," Nika muttered, rubbing her eyes. "If you ignore the whale guts."

Taria laughed and shook her head. "We're on our way to India now. A few more hours and we'll arrive."

While Nika's crew drifted through storms and seas inside their living vessel, another story unfolded across the waves. Charles's men had managed to find their stolen ship, repaired and readied, and were also cutting through the waters towards India.

On deck, Alex leaned on the rail, staring into the endless horizon. "It seems to me we need to sail not just to India... but beyond. To Tibet. To the Cloud Fairies. The last crystal will be there."

Lucas nodded. "Yes. That's where the book pointed."

"Then read it," Charles snapped from the helm. "Go through the pages. Tell me how to find it exactly."

Lucas pulled the weathered book from his bag and leafed nervously through the brittle pages. Symbols twisted and danced across the parchment. "It's... it's not very readable," he muttered, stalling.

"Not readable?" Charles stormed forward, his eyes blazing. He snatched the book out of Lucas's hands. "Do I have to do everything myself? No wonder that the witch laughed at you." His fingers moved quickly over the signs, his eyes narrowing in concentration. He flipped once, twice, and then stopped, his mouth curving into a sharp grin.

"I understand everything." He slammed the book shut.

Alex frowned. "Do you?"

"Yes," Charles growled. "I know how to find the last crystal. Raise the sails! Full speed ahead!"

The ship surged toward India, chasing the White Ghost and her companions once more.

Meanwhile, deep beneath the waves, Bubbles sailed to the Indian city Puri, near coast of India. With a shuddering groan, the whale tilted and spat the adventurers gently onto the sand. Soaked, tired, and yet alive, the crew stumbled onto dry land.

"Finally," Santigo muttered, kissing the beach. "I thought I'd die of nausea."

Nika turned back to the great whale and placed her hand on his skin. "Thank you, old friend. You've saved us again."

Bubbles let out a mournful, rumbling note, as though saying goodbye, then slide back into the ocean's depths.

The team turned inland. The road twisted through dense jungle, the cries of monkeys echoing overhead, until finally they reached a small village. On the hill above stood a wooden paddock, and inside—elephants.

Nika ran up the hill, her face breaking into a smile. She entered the small house and embraced a familiar man. "Nanda!" she said in Hindi. "How long has it been! How is Lucy? And little Kia? And your wife?"

The man's eyes lit up. "Nika! Whom I did not expect today, but how glad I am! My family is well. Kia has grown—strong and beautiful. Many wanted to buy him, but I refused. He cannot live without Lucy. And Lucy— she gave birth to two calves. Naira and Sita. Come, I'll show you."

Nika followed him to the paddock, where two tiny elephants played under their mother's shadow. "They're adorable," Nika whispered, petting them gently.

Taria's eyes widened, wonder sparkling in t hem. "How cute these land creatures are..." It was the first time she had ever seen elephants.

"So, Nika," Nanda said at last. "Why are you here?"

"I must get to Nepal," she explained, "and then to the Tibetan mountains. Urgently. Will you help me?"

"Of course," Nanda said without hesitation. "I will bring you my two fastest elephants, Shanti and Jay. They will carry you across India."

And so, once again, their journey began. For several days, they rode through jungles and plains, the mighty elephants carrying them onward.

Taria gasped at every new sight—the parrots bursting like flames through the trees, the golden temples shimmering in the sun, the endless rivers that coiled like snakes. For her, everything was new, everything a wonder.

Lorenzo, riding ahead, turned his head to Nika. "You've never told us," he said over the sound of the elephants' heavy steps, "how you got the power of air."

Nika's expression softened. She let the reins rest loose in her hands, the wind tugging at her hair.

"I suppose it's time you knew," she said quietly.

Ios, riding just behind, leaned in with a smile. He remembered those days—those sweet days—and his heart warmed as he waited for her tale.

Chapter 45: The Whisper of Air

"It was at the Ikuji temple in Nepal," Nika began, her voice carrying over the steady rhythm of the elephants' steps. "I found it... almost by accident, walking through the jungle. I didn't even know such a place existed. The first person I saw there was a monk named Sera. He jumped as if he'd seen a ghost. His eyes widened, his lips trembled, and in a whisper he asked me who I was, what I was doing there, and how I had gotten inside."

She paused, remembering that moment, and continued:

"I explained honestly—that I had simply wandered through the trees and stumbled upon the temple grounds. But he didn't look reassured. Instead, he grew pale and nervous. He told me I had to leave at once, immediately, because outsiders were forbidden to walk there. It was sacred ground, and no trespasser could remain."

The jungle wind blew against them, and even Taria, who had never seen temples of the land before, listened with wide-eyed wonder.

"But," Nika went on, "I couldn't leave. I had no idea where the entrance was, nor the exit. The paths of the temple grounds twisted like a labyrinth. Sera sighed, sighed, and decided to escort me himself. Even as he walked, he glanced around constantly, as if shadows were watching us. Finally, I asked him: 'Why are we hiding, and from whom?'"

She imitated the monk's quiet, urgent tone: "'This is sacred territory. Outsiders are forbidden here.'"

Her voice dropped. "That's when I saw him. In one of the side halls, seated alone, was a man whose entire body—his skin from head to toe—was covered in great green patches, swollen and sickly. I stopped in my tracks. He looked so frail, so hopeless. I turned to Sera and asked who he was.

'A hopelessly ill monk,' Sera told me, pulling at my sleeve. 'Nothing can save him. Come—we must hurry.'

But I couldn't. I told him, 'I can cure this man.'"

The team stirred at this point, leaning closer as if they too stood in that sacred hallway.

"Sera grew agitated, shaking his head. 'Impossible. You'll bring punishment upon us both if you linger. You must go.' He practically begged me to move faster, but even as he pulled me away, I swore that I would return."

Nika's eyes narrowed, as though she still felt the weight of that vow.

"I knew of a plant. High in the Himalayas grows a rare herb called Tiger's Claw. Its petals curl like talons, sharp and bloody-red. It is said to cure any sickness, man or beast, and fill the weak with renewed strength. But the hardest part..." She gave a small, ironic smile. "...was finding it."

The elephants were walking slowly, flapping their ears, as the group listened in silence.

"I climbed for days. Nights. Sometimes I thought the mountains wanted me dead. My hands were bloodied from the rocks, my lips cracked from the cold. But I pressed on. Then, one evening, I reached a ridge. Before me stretched the most beautiful sunset I had ever seen— colors of gold, fire, and violet flooding the horizon. I stood there too long, mesmerized... and I did not notice how close I had come to the edge."

Her voice grew softer, slower.

"One wrong step. The ground gave way. I slipped. I fell. Branches whipped me as I tumbled, rocks tore at my arms, and finally—I landed hard in the snow. For a while, I lay there, dazed, hardly breathing. Then... I heard it."

"What?" Santigo asked, almost whispering.

"The sound of wings," Nika said. "A great rustle, close and powerful, shaking the air. Something was there in the white silence of the mountain."

She drew in a slow breath, as if holding back the rest of the memory. But before she could go on, their elephant halted. Nanda raised a hand.

"I apologize for interrupting," Nanda said softly, "but we've reached the border of Tibet. Here the great mountain range begins."

Nika blinked, returning from her tale. She bowed her head to Nanda. "Thank you, old friend. Truly."

The team dismounted, staring up at the towering peaks. Spiked white crowns cut into the sky, icy winds sweeping down like knives. The road ahead looked dangerous, impossible.

"Where do we go from here?" Santigo asked uneasily.

Lorenzo wrapped his arms around himself, teeth already chattering. "We'll freeze in these clothes! We're not mountain goats. We'll die out there."

Nika just smiled faintly. She lifted her hands, and the air itself seemed to listen. She whispered a few words, and suddenly a whirlwind coiled around the group. Soft, invisible, it wrapped them like cloaks. The biting cold vanished. Their skin no longer burned from the wind, their breath no longer froze in their throats.

Lorenzo touched his chest, astonished. "What... was that? Why don't I feel cold anymore? What did you do to us?"

Nika's eyes glimmered with calm fire. "I used the gift of the air. With it, I can shield us from the cold. As long as we are bound together, no frost will touch you. We are safe—for now."

She turned toward the looming path of snow and stone, her cloak whipping in the wind.

"And now," she said, voice firm, "let's climb."

Taria hugged herself, staring at the impossible heights above them. Her voice trembled—not from cold, but from awesome. "It looks... incredible. But how do we even reach the top? Isn't it dangerous? I—I don't know if I'll be able to..."

Chapter 46: Mountains, Fairies and Snow

Nika raised her hands, her voice calm but firm, whispering an incantation that shimmered in the air like unseen threads. The spell wrapped around her companions like a breeze that wasn't there.

Taria blinked, puzzled. "What did you do? I don't feel any different."

"You will see," Nika replied with a knowing smile. "Go climb."

To Taria's astonishment, the moment her fingers touched the stone of the mountain wall, the climb felt easy—unnaturally so. Her arms moved as though weightless, her steps light as if gravity no longer clung so tightly to her. She looked back wide-eyed at the others.

"It's working," she whispered.

They climbed higher, the wind howling across the ridges, snowflakes whipping past their faces. Their cloaks swelled but no one shivered; Nika's spell had sealed away the cold.

On the narrow trail, Lorenzo glanced at her, remembering the interrupted tale from before. "You didn't finish your story," he called over the wind. "The one about how you got the power of air. What happened after you heard the wings in the forest?"

Nika's eyes softened as memories pulled her away from the present climb.

"As I said," she began, "in the forest I heard the rustle of wings, strange and haunting, as though the wind itself was alive. The cold was unbearable, my body numb. At last, I fell into the snow and everything went dark."

"But it turned out that forest wasn't ordinary. It was called the Forest of Death, because no one who entered ever returned. The reason... was the fairies. Snow fairies, guardians of the sky."

Her companions slowed to listen, even as their feet continued moving.

"One of them found me," Nika continued, "and carried me away. When I woke up, I was no longer on the mountain. I was in their city. Varideil."

Her voice took on reverence, almost awe.

"It wasn't just a city—it was thousands of cities, floating in the sky, all linked by silver air-bridges that shimmered like spider webs under the sun. The clouds beneath glowed like oceans of white, and the entire world stretched out below, distant and unreal. The fairies themselves were no taller than a meter, each with wings like spun glass, iridescent and ever-shifting. They hurried through their bridges and streets as though time themselves rushed them."

"By the seas…" Santigo muttered. "A city in the clouds…"

Nika nodded. "I stumbled outside, too stunned to believe it was real. I tried to leave, wandering to the outskirts— and that's when I realized the city floated thousands of kilometers above the earth. The abyss yawned beneath me."

She smiled faintly. "That's when Lucy appeared. She slipped up behind me, quiet as the breeze. She was the one who saved me in the forest. She smiled at me and said: 'Do you want to run away without even thanking me for saving your life?'

"I told her, of course not—that I was grateful beyond words. And she asked me what had brought me to the forest. I explained about the monk, the one with the green patches across his skin. How he was dying, and how I swore to heal him.

"When I described him, Lucy's eyes widened. She gasped and exclaimed: 'That is the Dalai Lama, the Seventh. The most enlightened monk I have ever known! He must not leave the earth—his time has not yet come. Now I understand why you were led here. You must have been seeking the Tiger's Claw.'"

Nika's eyes glittered as she recited Lucy's words.

"Then she took my hand and said she would help me. She led me through Varideil, into their sacred hall. Imagine a chamber of crystal glass, soaring and endless, filled with thousands of plants sealed in vessels of shining quartz. It was their living archive of the world's rarest herbs. Each one glowed faintly, nourished by pure starlight. And there—she found it. The Tiger's Claw."

The group was silent, captured by the vision.

"But as we left," Nika said, her voice dropping, "we met the guards. They had discovered me, a trespasser in their holy city. They chased us, their wings slicing the air, their voices like whistles of a storm. Lucy and I ran, twisting through bridges of light, the abyss yawning below us. The guards closed in. There was no way forward, only the edge of the floating city. No way back either.

"And then—she pushed me."

"What?!" Taria gasped.

"I fell," Nika said softly. "The sky swallowed me, the ground rushing up from far, far below. I screamed. My heart stopped. And then... she dove after me. I felt her wings beside me, heard her whisper in my ear: 'Do not be afraid. Everything will be fine.'

"She breathed onto me, and I felt it—a warm breath of wind, scented with almonds. The air itself wrapped around me. 'Now you have the magic of air,' she said. 'Use it.' She gave me the herb, smiled, and flew away... vanishing into the storm."

Nika spread her hands as if reliving that moment.

"I was falling still, but something inside me had changed. The air bent to my will. Scared, not knowing what to do—but it answered me. It held me. My fall slowed. My body grew light as a feather. And then... I landed safely on the earth, the Tiger's Claw still in my hands."

There was silence among the group. The wind moaned across the ridges, but no one spoke.

Finally, Santigo cleared his throat. "Wait... you mean you can actually fly?"

Nika gave a small smile. "Yes."

Chapter 47: The Breath of the Mountains

"I returned to the temple," Nika continued, her voice low and thoughtful as they climbed, "and found Sera. I gave him the Tiger's Claw and explained carefully how to prepare and use it. Sera trusted me—he truly did—but even so, he feared. He wanted to be sure the plant would heal, not harm.

"So he brought the herb before the council of elders. There lived in the temple a creature most unusual: a tame lynx. Not an ordinary animal, but one that the monks believed was born under a sacred star. She had an uncanny gift—to sense poisons in any form, and more than that, to see the truth in men's intentions. For centuries, the monks relied on her judgment when their own wisdom faltered."

Taria leaned forward on her elephant, hanging on every word. Even Lorenzo, who often masked his fascination with sarcasm, listened intently.

"The lynx was led into the council hall," Nika went on. "Silent paws against the stone. Her amber eyes glowed like small suns. They set the Tiger's Claw before her. She circled it once, twice, sniffing... then she leapt back suddenly, her body low and her fur bristling, as though she felt the power hidden in the plant. But instead of growing in warning, she lowered her head to the ground."

Nika's eyes glimmered as she relived the moment. "It was a bow. A sign of acceptance."

"And the monks believed her?" asked Santigo skeptically, though his voice had softened.

"One of the oldest monks stepped forward. He took the plant reverently in his wrinkled hands, bowed to the lynx, then nodded to Sera. 'Where did you get this herb?' he demanded.

"Sera could not lie. Trembling, he told them the truth—that I had brought it, and that I still remained within the temple walls, though no stranger was allowed. He begged forgiveness."

Nika paused, and Lorenzo leaned forward impatiently. "Well? What happened then?"

"The elder ordered them to bring me before the council. I was led into the great hall, torches flickering, the monks' eyes all upon me. And before any words were spoken, the lynx approached me. Slowly. She sniffed my robes, my hands, even my hair. Then she locked her eyes with mine, golden fire meeting my own gaze.

"And then," Nika smiled faintly, "she roared—not in anger, but like thunder rolling across the mountains—and bowed her head to me, just as she had to the Tiger's Claw."

Lorenzo let out a sharp breath. "And what did the monks do? Pray tell, they didn't bow to you as well?"

"They did," Nika said softly. "The Senior Monk turned to the assembly and declared aloud: 'A pure soul!' Then he bowed to me. One by one, the others followed."

For a moment, even Santigo was struck dumb. Finally, he burst out, shaking his head: "Nothing but a sailor's fancy! By Neptune's beard, lass, you tell tales taller than the mainmast!"

But Taria's eyes shone. "No, Santigo. Her adventures are so interesting, so unusual... they carry the ring of truth."

"So how did it end?" Lorenzo asked, his tone half-teasing, half-earnest.

Nika's smile grew wistful. "Very simply. The Dalai Lama was given a potion brewed from the Tiger's Claw. His strength returned. The spots faded. He rose and thanked me himself. He told me that from that day forward, the temple doors would always be open to me. And more—he said it would be his honor to teach me the sacred knowledge, if ever I chose to stay and learn."

Ios, riding just behind, smiled quietly. "That is indeed our Nika."

"Yes," Lorenzo admitted, stroking his chin, "I'll grant you that much... but one thing still troubles me. Why did the fairies' guards chase you in Varideil? Why such hatred?"

Nika's face grew somber. "Because Lucy's sister, the fairy queen, despises humankind. She sees only greed, spite, and cruelty in people. She passed a law that forbade any fairy from touching, helping, or even speaking to a human. The punishment was... severe. Any fairy who defied the law was turned into dust—earth and nothing more. Lucy..." Nika's voice trembled just slightly, "...Lucy was kind. Braver than most. She often broke her sister's laws. I fear for her. I only hope she still lives."

Silence followed, heavy as the mountain mist.

By then the travelers had reached a narrow pass. The wind shrieked between the rocks, and the first stars pricked the darkening sky. The cold was sharpening; each breath felt like glass in the lungs. Even the spell was weak for this kind of cold.

"We'll freeze if we press on," said Lorenzo, rubbing his arms. "Even with your magic, Nika, we need shelter."

Taria pointed ahead, her eyes brightening. "Look there! A cave. Doesn't it look... like the head of a wolf?"

Indeed, the jagged rocks framed an entrance shaped like snarling jaws, the shadows inside as black as a predator's throat.

"Let's spend the night there," she suggested.

"Great idea," Ios agreed, tightening his cloak.

The team went towards the eerie cave. Inside, the air was warmer, sheltered from the wind, though the dripping of unseen water echoed through the cavern. They set down, lit a fire, and the glow flickered across the rough stone walls—shadows stretching long, like the teeth of a wolf waiting to bite.

They stopped in the cave, its entrance like the gaping maw of a wolf, and the cold mountain wind howled through the stones. Shadows danced as Lorenzo and Ios rekindled a bonfire from half-dry branches, sparks leaping like fireflies into the blackness of night. The warmth spread slowly, but the cave was vast, and it seemed as though darkness was always pressed closer, eager to smother the light.

Taria, sitting cross-legged by the fire, broke the silence.

"What are we going to do next?" she asked softly, her voice carrying both curiosity and unease.

Nika leaned forward, her face illuminated in gold and crimson by the flames.

"Because Charles has the book and he's walking along our path, we have to hurry. Taria, do you remember how to activate the crystals, so they would show us the way to the temple?"

Taria nodded, her eyes glowing with determination.

"Yes. I remember the last pages very well. Every symbol, every word is etched in my mind."

"Good." Nika reached for the leather satchel and placed it carefully in Taria's lap, as though it contained not stones, but the beating heart of the world itself. "Then I'll leave you this bag with crystals. Keep your eyes on them and promise me—if I don't come back in three days— you must take these crystals to the bottom of the sea and hide them in the safest place. No one must find them. And if anyone tries to interfere or steal them from you, use your powers. Remember this, it's important. The fate of the world is in your hands now."

The fire crackled, throwing sparks into the cave roof, and Ios leaned forward, stunned.

"Whhhh... what are you going to do?" he asked, his voice trembling slightly.

Nika stood, her shadow stretching long and tall against the jagged wall.

"I'm going to fly to the fairies for the last crystal. Right now. And the night will help me with this."

The team exchanged looks of alarm.

Chapter 48: The city of Varideil

"Are you going to do it without us?" Lorenzo asked, his voice a mixture of protest and hurt.

"Yes," Nika replied firmly, though her eyes softened. "For one simple reason: you can't fly. You would only be a burden. And besides—I need all of you here. We are a team, and I remember that very well. I need you safe, I need you strong. If I fail, the crystals are all that matter."

Before anyone could argue further, her form shimmered, dissolved into the night air, and disappeared in front of them.

She flew swiftly toward the cloud cities of the winged creatures, her body lifted by currents of wind, her heart pounding. Moonlight guided her path, and stars scattered like silver dust across the heavens. But no sooner had she crossed into their skies, than blinding spears of light shot upward. Fairy guards, their wings sharp as blades, intercepted her.

"Seize her!" one barked.

They caught her in a net woven from starlight and bound her, dragging her down into the heart of their kingdom. She was cast into a magical dungeon, its walls shimmering with runes that shimmered like frozen lightning. Here, no spell could take root, no magic could breathe. The very air was dead.

Word spread quickly. The queen, merciless and proud, was informed at once. She despised humans, despised their greed and cruelty, and when she heard Nika's name her cold smile widened.

"Tomorrow, at dawn, she will be executed," the queen decreed. "But first—put Holie on her."

The bracelets, silver bands glowing faintly, were clasped on Nika's wrists. Instantly her heart felt heavy, her eyes dulled, her will itself seemed stolen. Holie did not just bind the body—it shackled the soul, blocking any emotion.

In the throne room, among the courtiers, Lucy was present. Her blood froze at the queen's words. She alone knew the risk, the cruelty, and the injustice of it. She clenched her fists, wings trembling with urgency. There was no time to waste.

That night, as silence wrapped the kingdom, Lucy slipped unseen through the marble corridors. She reached the dungeon, pushed past the guards with a whisper of invisibility magic, and entered the cell.

"I cannot believe it! Nika, Nika—it's me, Lucy!"

Nika sat slumped against the wall, her eyes empty, her face pale as ash. Lucy bent down, shook her gently.

"Don't you recognize me?" she appeals.

Nika lifted her gaze, but it was hollow, like a puppet with its strings cut.

Lucy gasped softly. "Of course... it's the bracelets. Holie has drained you." Her jaw set in determination. "Wait for me. I'll return."

Lucy raced across the city, her wings shining in the moonlight, until she reached the Great Library—the largest in all the fairy realms. Inside, columns of crystal rose high into the skies, and shelves wound like mazes. She moved quickly, past endless corridors of scrolls and tomes, until she reached a secret chamber, marked with a single letter carved into the arch: K.

From her pocket she drew a tiny key. With trembling hands she unlocked the hidden door and stepped inside. On the shelf lay a small chest, ancient and ornate, sealed with seven silver locks. Whispering an incantation, she opened it. Inside was a thin golden plate, etched with the ancient runes of release. The spell to shatter Holie's curse.

She hurried back, every heartbeat echoing like thunder in her chest. Back in the dungeon, she knelt before Nika and lifted the plate. The words carved upon it glowed faintly, almost alive. Lucy began to recite:

"Domin iha hao, soi bin iha be, ria dao que, ria dao see, soriorika soriokia. Pori kii bei, zori jiji nei, imebino imecino vio dio kei..."

As soon as Lucy finished reading it, the bracelets turned into dust and disappeared. Nika woke up. However, she was still in the dungeon, she had to find the way out. Only a couple of hours left before fairies would execute her.

"Don't worry, I'll help you." Lucy said.

The fairy cast another spell, and with a faint shimmer of silver dust, the dungeon door creaked open. Nika leapt forward, her heart swelling, and embraced Lucy. The warmth of the fairy's touch brought her courage back, though the cold stone around them reminded her how little time they had left.

"Lucy," Nika whispered, clutching her tightly. "I'm so glad to see you—and thank you, thank you again for saving me."

Lucy smiled, but her voice was urgent. "No time for thanks. It's almost dawn, and if they find you here..." She didn't finish, but her trembling wings and a quick glance toward the barred window told Nika all she needed to know.

The fairy waved her hand again, casting a minor charm that made the air shimmer. Two guards at the corridor turned their heads, distracted by a phantom sound echoing in the distance. At that very moment, Nika darted out of the dungeon, slipping past unseen.

But she stopped. "Lucy—I can't leave without the crystal. It's the last one. I already have all the others."

Lucy froze mid-flight, astonishment flickering across her face. "What are you talking about? A crystal? What crystal?"

"Run with me," Nika said, grabbing her hand. "I'll tell you on the way."

Chapter 49: Kiki and little transformation

The two dart through narrow, spiraling streets where triangular houses extended out like jagged teeth. The moonlight spilled across bridges of glass, and the whole city of clouds glowed faintly blue in the night. Nika spoke between breaths, her voice low and quick.

"I found the book 'Nouveau,'" she explained. "It led me through the seas, deserts, dragons, and now here. Every crystal belongs to one element, and the last—air—must be here, with your people."

Lucy's wings faltered for a moment as she hovered. She looked at Nika as though seeing her anew. "The Temple of the Seven Seas? That's... that's a child's tale."

"I thought so too," Nika answered, her eyes burning with intensity. "But it's real. The book guided me, and I've seen things that no tale could invent."

Something in Nika's tone—honest, fierce, unwavering—cut through Lucy's doubt. The fairy understood. This girl was not lying.

Lucy's expression hardened. "Then we'll need help. Run with me to Kiki. She can do what others cannot."

They wove between shadowed lanes, darting past fairy patrols, until at last they reached a small crooked house wedged between two towers of crystal. A crooked sign swayed in the wind: Kiki's Curiosities.

Lucy banged on the carved wooden door. "Kiki! Open up—it's me!"

There was a long pause, then a muffled, sleepy voice replied, "What is it? Who disturbs me at this hour?"

The door opened with a groan, revealing a small fairy with wild hair and huge, round glasses sliding down her nose. She blinked, rubbing her eyes—then froze.

"Lucy... what is that behind you? Tell me I'm not seeing... a human?" Her wings twitched nervously. She inhaled sharply, ready to scream.

Lucy darted forward and covered her mouth. "Hush! Don't scream. She's with me. She's my friend. And she needs our help."

181

Kiki buzzed erratically around the room, bumping into shelves stacked with jars and glowing bottles. "Help? With what?! Do you know what happens if the Queen finds out? Do you like being turned into dust?"

Lucy grabbed her by the shoulders. "Please, Kiki. We need her to pass as one of us. Only you can disguise her. Dress her, hide her, make her look like a real fairy. Without it, she won't survive until morning."

Kiki's large eyes darted from Lucy to Nika. She groaned dramatically, wings flapping like agitated fans. "Fine, fine. Bring her in. But if we're caught, my shop's cursed forever and so am I!"

She tugged Nika inside and dragged her toward a cluttered dressing chamber full of shimmering silks, wing-caps, and enchanted ornaments. Minutes passed as Kiki fussed and flitted about. At last, she stepped back, proud of her work.

Even Lucy gasped. Nika no longer looked human—her hair was woven with threads of starlight, her clothes shimmered with delicate patterns of feathers and frost, her skin faintly glowed as though touched by moonlight.

"The only thing missing is the wings," Lucy whispered.

Kiki tapped her chin, then grinned slyly. "Ah, wings... tricky, tricky. But not impossible." She looked through a tall cabinet, tossing aside bottles that fizzed, smoked, or squeaked. Finally, she pulled out two small glass vials.

"I have a potion that can restore a broken wing... or grow one anew. It's unstable, but it works." Her grinned, mischievous and a little wicked. "If you're brave enough, human."

Nika raised an eyebrow. "And how do I get rid of them later? I don't plan to spend the rest of my life pretending to be something I'm not."

"Ha! Clever girl," Kiki giggled. She held up another vial. "This one's the antidote. Purple to grow wings, green to take them away. Just don't mix them up—or who knows what you'll become."

The bottles glowed faintly in her hands, one swirling like violet storm clouds, the other bubbling like liquid emerald fire.

Nika reached for them slowly, her heart pounding. She felt the weight of her journey pressing on her shoulders. If this gamble failed, her quest—and perhaps her life— would end in the fairies' city before dawn.

Lucy leaned close, whispering, "It's your choice, Nika. But if you're to reach the crystal, you must take the risk."

Chapter 50: The Risk and the Library

Nika raised the purple vial to her lips. The liquid shimmered like liquid dawn, sweet and heavy, coating her tongue as though it carried hidden sparks. She drained it in one gulp, and a moment later, her eyelids fluttered. A sudden drowsiness overtook her, followed by a prickling itch across her back. She gasped as warmth spread through her shoulders, and in an instant—they burst forth.

Large, pearl-pink wings unfurled from her back, translucent and alive, with a golden-yellow overflow like molten sunlight on water. They shimmered when she moved, leaving faint trails of light in the air.

Lucy clapped her hands together, eyes wide in awe. "So beautiful... I have never seen such wings, not even among my kind. They are... radiant."

Nika turned her head slightly, watching them catch the light, surprised by their elegance. "They feel... natural. As if they were always meant to be mine."

She tucked the green vial carefully into her pouch and bowed her head to Kiki. "Thank you—for this and more. I'll return it when the time comes."

Kiki sniffed, pretending not to be touched, though her wings quivered. "Just don't get yourself killed before you bring it back. My potions deserve better than to vanish with their drinkers."

With no time to waste, Nika and Lucy leapt into the air, their wings cutting through the night. The city below glittered faintly, but the glow of the great Library drew them like a beacon.

Inside, the Library of the Fairies was unlike any other place Nika had seen. Endless shelves of crystal and frost rose in spirals that seemed to defy gravity, filled with glowing tomes, whispering scrolls, and floating maps that rearranged themselves when touched. The silence there was heavy, not dead, but sacred—as though each word ever written hovered in the air, watching.

"Why here?" Nika asked as they flew between spiraling shelves. "Why the library?"

Lucy's eyes flickered around nervously, scanning for patrolling scribes. "Because it holds every book, every fragment, every secret of the world. If the crystal is truly part of the story, you say... perhaps there's a record of it here. But—"

Nika raised her hand. "Shh."

Her heart skipped. A melody, faint but clear, had entered her head again—like flutes playing underwater. The notes were soft, insistent, and they pulled her as surely as the tide.

Lucy noticed her freeze. "Why did we stop?"

"The sound," Nika whispered. "It's calling from here. Behind this wall."

Lucy blinked at the expanse of blank ice-crystal before them. "What are you talking about? It's just a wall."

Nika pressed her palm flat against it, feeling its cool smoothness. She narrowed her eyes, searching—and there, barely visible, a mark: a tiny triangle etched in faint frost. She touched it. The world dropped away.

Her body fell forward into a void, the air rushing around her ears, until her hand brushed something cold and metallic. A ring. Instinctively, she pulled.

"Carefully!" Lucy squeaked, wings flaring as the wall shuddered and began to collapse inward.

Stone and ice dissolved into motes of light, revealing a staircase winding steeply downward. The music swelled, no longer only in Nika's head—now Lucy heard it too.

Her eyes went wide. "What is that? I hear it too... that sound—it's... otherworldly."

"Yes," Nika said, her voice low, reverent. "And I think I know what it is."

They descended quickly. The stairs narrowed, turning into a low passage. The glow of flickering yellow light sawed from the tunnel's depths, and the melody became stronger, more insistent, as if calling them.

"We'll have to crawl," Nika muttered, peering ahead. "There's no other way."

Lucy hesitated, wings trembling. "And what if it's nothing? Or worse, a trap laid for us?"

Nika's expression is hardened. "Then you can wait here, Lucy. I won't ask you to risk yourself for me. But I—" her hand pressed against her chest—"I must finish what I started."

Lucy's hesitation lasted only a breath. She crawled forward after Nika. "I won't leave you. Not now."

For what felt like hours, they wriggled through the tunnel, cold stone scraping their hands, wings tucked tightly against their backs. The melody grew louder, clearer—hunting yet beautiful.

At last, the tunnel opened onto a wide platform of pure ice, glowing like a mirror. Nika gasped, for before them stood a hall unlike any they had seen: triangular in shape, its walls carved entirely from glacial white crystal. From the ceiling to the floor descended a colossal ice-drop, frozen in eternal mid-fall.

And inside it—glowing like the trapped sun—was the yellow crystal. Its light radiated through the hall, scattering golden beams that danced like living fire across the ice.

Lucy's breath caught. "By the stars..."

Drawn by awe, she fluttered closer. Her fingers brushed the crystal—and instantly seared. "Aaaah! Hot!" She jerked back, clutching her hand.

"Lucy!" Nika cried. "Don't touch it—it's meant for me."

Summoning her courage, Nika soared upward. The melody filled her veins now, encouraging her on. She reached out and gripped the crystal. Fire and wind roared through her body. Her wings beat once—twice—and in a flash of light, she vanished.

"Farewell, Nika," Lucy whispered, eyes wide but relieved. "May you succeed."

The world spun, and Nika found herself stumbling onto soft earth. She blinked, finding herself in a quiet forest. The air smelled of pine and rain, the crystal heavy in her hand. Her wings still glimmered faintly in the dawn light.

She looked at the green vial. "Time to put these away," she murmured, raising it to her lips.

Part VII: The Temple

Chapter 51: The Price of Light

The antidote was bitter, sharp against her tongue, and for a moment she thought it had no effect. But then, a familiar itch returned, crawling across her shoulders. She gasped as the pearl-pink wings dissolved into mist and were drawn back into her skin. Nika reached behind her back instinctively—only smooth flesh remained.

"They're gone," she whispered to herself, though her voice carried relief and an unspoken sadness. "Thank you, Lucy... for everything."

She slipped the empty vial away just as a voice struck her mind like a thunderclap:

"Nika! Help! Hurry!"

It was Taria's voice—sharp, desperate, telepathic.

Her heart started pounding heavily. Clutching the glowing crystal in her hand, she sprinted towards the source of the call. The wind rose under her feet, lifting her swifter than she imagined, carrying her straight to the cave where they had last camped.

The scene she entered was chaos.

Charles and his men had found them. Smoke and sparks filled the cave as steel clashed, shouts echoed, and the air reeked of fire and blood. Santigo swung his cutlass furiously against Lucas, while Lorenzo fought off two mercenaries at once. Taria stood near the crystals, she could not summon the water, so she was sitting in the corner watching the fight.

At the entrance, Charles himself stood waiting. His eyes were wild, his revolver steady. And as soon as he saw Nika appear in the doorway, crystal in hand, his lips curled into a cruel grin.

"Witch," he spat, and fired.

The crack of the gunshot shattered the fight. Nika's eyes widened—too fast to dodge, no time to shield herself.

But then—

Ios!

He lunged forward, placing himself between her and the bullet. The sound echoed like thunder in the hollow cave. His body jerked with the impact, and he collapsed into her arms, blood spreading quickly across his chest.

The entire cavern froze. No one moved. No one breathed.

"Ios..." Nika whispered, trembling. She pressed her hand to his wound, but the light in his eyes faded even as he smiled faintly. "I couldn't... let them... take you..." His body fell limp.

"Nooooo!" Nika's cry echoed, tearing through stone.

Lorenzo's rage ignited. He ripped his saber from its sheath and with one furious strike, cut Charles down. The villain's revolver clattered to the ground, his eyes wide in disbelief as he collapsed lifeless beside the cave wall.

But Nika's voice cut through the silence, stronger than the storm.

"Stop! Enough! No more fighting!" She got up slowly, clutching the crystal to her chest. Her voice trembled with grief but carried iron. "No more blood. We are not enemies. We must not be."

Alex, pale and shaking, snarled, "You are a witch!"

Before he could spit another word, Taria strode forward and slapped him hard across the face. Her voice was fierce as steel. "Stop it now. You've no idea who you're talking to."

Nika's eyes burned as she looked between Alex and Lucas. "I gave you my trust. I shared my knowledge with you as a sister. And you betrayed me—for a man who only used you. Can't you see? Charles was going to throw you away the moment you weren't useful. Open your eyes, Alex! Lucas! The choice is yours: with me, or alone in the dark."

Her words trembled like thunder.

Lorenzo stepped beside her, his voice deep and resolute. "She's right. Nika... she's not like anyone else. She's brave, clever, selfless—she would lay down her life for us, for her family. What did Charles ever give you but fear and empty promises?"

Alex faltered, breathing hard. "He... he gave me..." His voice broke. "I—I can't even remember anymore." He bowed his head, muttering something too low to hear.

Lucas said nothing, but his eyes softened, the conflict cleared in his face.

Then Santigo, bloodied but unbroken, slammed his blade into the earth. "Enough speeches. Stop talking. We've wasted too much time already. Let's find this cursed temple and end it!"

Nika looked at Ios's body one last time, grief carving lines in her face. "We will... but his sacrifice will not be in vain."

She lifted the worn book from the ground. Its cover was warm under her fingers, humming faintly with magic. She flipped it open—only to see… emptiness. Every page is blank.

"What? No... no!" She frantically turned page after page, her eyes wide. "Where are the words? Where is the text? What happened to the book?"

Lucas stepped forward, suspicion thick in his voice. "What have you done?"

"Nothing! I swear I didn't touch it—why is it gone?"

Lorenzo slammed his fist against the cave wall. "Is this another trick, Nika? Don't play with us now!"

"I didn't do anything!" she shouted, tears in her eyes.

Taria placed her hand gently over the book. Her voice was calm, steady. "Do not be afraid. I know why it's blank. The book is not ordinary. It feels the soul of its master. For too long it was corrupted in the hands of Charles—greedy, cruel, unworthy. And so, the book closed itself, hiding its knowledge. Words will never appear for the undeserving."

Her eyes flickered to Nika. "But we don't need it anymore. I remember the final pages. The path is still clear."

She turned to the crystals. "Nika, take them out. Lay them before you, and join them together as one."

Nika's hands trembled as she obeyed, placing the four crystals carefully in the sand. She tried to connect them—pushing, rotating, fitting edges like a puzzle. Half an hour passed, sweat beading on her forehead, but nothing happened.

Her grief boiled into anger. "Why won't you work!?" she cried. In frustration, she hurled the stones against the wall.

Chapter 52: The Temple of Seven Seas

The crystals clattered across the floor… then froze in midair.

With a sudden surge of light, they spun together, edges aligning with perfect precision. A single radiant crystal formed—blazing with blinding white brilliance. The cavern filled with pure light, so bright that the team shielded their eyes. The ground rumbled, the walls shook, and in a heartbeat—

They were no longer in the cave.

Nika opened her eyes and gasped.

They stood on polished marble, in a hall so vast it stretched beyond sight. Pillars of coral rose around them, waterfalls of light cascading down walls of crystal. The air shimmered with the scent of salt and eternity.

Before them, carved into the floor itself, lay a sigil glowing with all the colors of the seas.

"The Temple of the Seven Seas," Taria whispered, awe and reverence in her voice.

Nika clutched the unified crystal tightly, her heart pounding.

"How... did we get here?" Lorenzo breathed, his saber still in his hand, eyes wide with disbelief.

Nika's voice was hushed, trembling with wonder. "The crystals brought us. The temple has accepted us."

"Nika, what did you do?" Lucas exclaimed, his voice trembling between awe and panic.

"Humans, I'll explain everything to you later. We are where we should be. Look there," Taria said, pointing with her slender hand toward the door.

Before them loomed a 20-meter-high structure—a massive door forged entirely of purple-blue metal. It shimmered like liquid light, as though it were suspended in the air, untouched by gravity. The glow was so radiant that the team felt their eyes being drawn into it, unable to look away. It pulsed like a living heart, humming with ancient power.

Lucas, Alex, and Lorenzo with Santigo were the first to dash toward it. They pressed their hands against the surface, straining their muscles to pull the door open.

"That's all we need!" Lorenzo shouted, gripping the handle with all his strength. His veins bulged, his jaw clenched—but the door did not budge.

It stood still, eternal, unmoved by human effort.

Then Nika approached. With steady hands, she drew out the unified crystal, its blinding white core now shifting into every color of the rainbow at once. She slide it into the lock. To their amazement, the jagged shape of the crystal aligned perfectly with the carved hollow.

With a low, thunderous rumble, the door opened. Beyond it unfolded the Temple of the Seven Seas.

Suddenly, an otherworldly figure appeared—the God of Light. His brilliance flooded the chamber, so radiant that the heroes were instantly blinded. Their screams echoed in the great hall as a soundless force, like an invisible wave, swept over them. One by one, they were torn apart from each other, lifted by beams of energy, and hurled into separate mirror-rooms.

Chapter 53: The Trial of Reflections

When they awoke, confusion reigned.

The rooms were endless, covered in mirrors on the walls, the floor, and even the ceiling. Each reflection moved in unison at first, mimicking their every breath and step. But the more the heroes struggled, the stranger it became. The reflections began to break rhythm—smiling when they did not, sneering, whispering words they never spoke. Soon, the whispers grew louder, multiplying, crawling inside their minds.

Shadows flickered. Hallucinations bled into reality. Fears that had been buried deep within their hearts came alive before their eyes.

…Let's look at each of the Trial shall we…

Lucas pressed his hands against the mirrored walls, desperate to break through. But each reflection turned cruel, eyes glowing with a sickly green light. He saw himself drowning in a stormy sea, thrashing for breath as phantom hands pulled him under.

"You'll never rise above the waves," the voices hissed.

"You betrayed Nika. You betrayed your friends. Treachery is in your blood."

"I didn't have a choice!" Lucas shouted, but the water surged higher, filling his lungs. He coughed, sputtered, clawing at nothing.

The reflections laughed, whispered: "Coward. Always choosing the easier tide. Always swimming away from the fight."

Lucas fell to his knees, tears burning his eyes. "No... not this time. Not anymore. I'll fight—I'll fight for them." He slammed his fist into the mirror, and for the briefest moment, a crack of light appeared.

Chapter 54: The Struggle

Alex's chamber was a study without doors—walls crowded with charts, star maps, and neat rows of knives. In every mirror he saw himself older, colder, a ledger in one hand and a string of marionette wire in the other. Reflections tugged the wires, and people danced: Nika, Lorenzo, Lucas… even Alex himself.

"You only matter when you're in control," the reflections murmured.

"Better to pull the strings than be cut by them."

"Trust is a coin you spend once. Power buys safety."

Across the room a vision flickered: Nika reached for him as a storm closed in. In Alex's hand, the book—glittering with answers. He watched his mirrored self choose the book and let Nika fall.

Alex's jaw clenched. "That's not who I want to be."

The mirrors laughed—a dry, papery sound. "Want is wind. Choice is steel."

Wires tightened around his wrists. He felt the old hunger: to be the smartest in the room, the one who couldn't be betrayed because he'd already anticipated it. He saw Alex-the-Strategist, the boy who learned early that affection had terms and mercy had a cost.

He shut his eyes. "I've been jealous. Of her courage. Of Lorenzo's certainty. I hid behind plans because I was afraid of failing them." He raised his bound hands. "No more."

He pulled—not at the wires, but at the knot inside his chest. The marionette lines slackened, then snapped. The reflections faltered.

"I choose people over power," he said, voice steady. "And if that breaks me, then I'll break honest."

…Lorenzo, Lorenzo…

Steel clashed in Lorenzo's chamber. His reflection stood before him, dressed as a blood-soaked pirate captain, saber dripping red. The mirrored Lorenzo grinned, stepping forward.

"This is who you are," it sneered.

"A killer. A thief. Nothing but scum of the seas. Do you think Nika truly trusts you? You'll betray her the moment it suits you—just as you've betrayed others."

Lorenzo's grip tightened on his saber. "No. That life is behind me."

"Behind you?" the reflection laughed, slashing at him. Their blades met with a thunderous clang. "It is you. The sea will always call you back. Blood will always stain your hands."

The real Lorenzo roared, parrying strike after strike, until he finally disarmed his reflection. "I am not the man I was. I fight now for something greater—for her... for us all." He drove the blade into the mirror, and the bloody figure shattered into fragments.

…When it came to Santigo, he was tired, half blooded and lost…

Santigo's mirrored chamber filled with laughter— mocking, cruel, endless. He saw himself dressed in rags, chained before a crowd of jeering faces.

"Nothing but a fool," they chanted.

"Clown, jester, worthless shadow. Why do you even follow them? You are no hero. You're dead weight. Always the weak link."

Santigo gritted his teeth, his fists shaking. "Maybe I'm not as strong as the others. Maybe I joke too much. But I'll never abandon them. I'd rather be a fool who fights with heart than a coward who runs."

The chains shattered, the crowd vanished, and Santigo stood taller than he ever had before.

…From all of these pirates Taria, the daughter of the Atlantis, had a pure heart and soul… She hasn't done anything wrong in her life…Or I only thought that way?

Taria's mirror warped, twisting her reflection into a monstrous mermaid—skin pale, eyes hollow, teeth like jagged coral.

"You failed your kingdom," the creature hissed, circling her. "Your people are gone. You couldn't save them. You call yourself a princess, but you are nothing. A fraud."

"You went chasing the Temple? Ha!"

"You left your people, you left your father."

Taria trembled. "No... I—I did all I could. I couldn't stop the war, I couldn't stop the flood—"

"Excuses," the reflection snarled, dragging her toward the water that began rising around them. "You are weak. You were never fit to rule. That's why the sea swallowed your people."

For a moment, despair weighed her down. But then, remembering Nika's courage, Taria clenched her fists. "No! I may have lost my home…They are waiting for me…I will return…

And Nika—Nika's ordeal was the cruelest of all.

Her reflections multiplied until thousands of Nikas stood before her, their voices rising into a storm:

"You are not chosen. You are an accident."

"You never saved anyone—you only bring destruction."

"Your friends follow you only because they are blind."

"Your power is borrowed. Your destiny is hollow."

She raised her hands, calling on her magic. Flames burst from her palms, water swirled around her, air and earth trembled at her command. But the more she cast spells, the more the illusions multiplied, feeding off her energy like parasites. The fire she conjured burned her skin, the water tried to drown her, the air choked her, and the earth threatened to swallow her whole.

Her knees buckled. Her heart pounded.

"I'm doing something wrong," she whispered, clenching her fists. "There must be another way... an exit... a truth."

But the spirits hissed from every corner, from every reflection:

"There is no other way."

"Give up."

"You are just a little mortal."

"You imagine you are special—but in the end, you are worthless, like the thousands of others before you."

The room pulsed with their taunts, the sound hammering in her ears. For the first time in a long while, fear clawed at Nika's heart.

Chapter 55: Nika's Trial

"Why are you trying to get out of here?"

"So why are you even trying to save the world, which tomorrow will forget you?"

"Who are you trying to prove it?"

"Everyone lives their own life, no one needs you."

"And now everyone is thinking about their miserable life, how to save it."

"And you, you think about how to get out from here too."

"No... it's not true," Nika objected, her voice trembling but stubborn. "They are my friends..."

"Are you dear to them?" the reflections sneered, their faces stretching and warping into cruel masks of her own image.

And then, something clicked inside her. A sudden clarity.

"I understand now," she said, smiling faintly. "This is brilliant... thank you very much."

Her reflections froze, staring at her with cold, endless eyes.

"Stupid princess," they hissed. "Inappropriately raised, careless, naive. We are your true self, your shadows, your fears, your secrets."

Nika tilted her head, chuckled softly, and answered:

"Ha ha, how frightening you sound. But you're only smoke. Illusions. You don't exist. I see through your trick."

But the whisperers pressed closer, surrounding her like a swarm.

"It seems the king was wrong not to marry you to Charles. At least you would be obedient, silent, tamed."

"You are nothing but a pitiful girl pretending to be a pirate."

"A coward hiding under brave words."

"She can't even spell, can't even lead."

"Weak."

"Always dressed in rags like a beggar."

"A spoiled little princess chasing fairy tales."

The voices grew faster, harsher, overlapping like an endless storm.

"It was because of you that Ios was killed! If you had respected your friends, if you weren't so reckless, so drunk on your adventures, he would still be alive."

"The blood of Ios is on your hands."

"Selfish!"

"Hypocrite!"

"Miserable!"

The accusations pounded against her chest like hammers. For a moment, her knees buckled. But then she drew a deep breath, straightened, and spoke:

"Alright. You had your turn. Now it's mine."

She spread her arms, as though addressing the whole universe.

"You know, while we waste time here with your venomous chatter, stars are being born. Entire solar systems swirl into existence. Galaxies collide and blossom into new light. Compared to those miracles, your noise is nothing. And besides—" she smirked, "you are not real. You are just shadows in my mind. I am in control of my thoughts, not you. And now I command you—vanish."

She stamped her foot so hard the mirrors trembled.

"GET OUT!" she roared, her voice splitting the air like thunder.

Silence fell. The whispers evaporated into nothing. The countless reflections around her flickered, warped, and then cracked like glass shattering.

She stood panting, eyes burning with tears, but whispered fiercely:

"I love my friends. My family…With all my heart. That is who I am. That is my truth."

Her strength gave out. She collapsed onto the floor, falling into a deep, dreamless sleep.

Chapter 56: Teatime with Gods

When her eyes opened again, she was no longer in the mirrored prison. She sat on a vast white floor that shimmered like marble but had no end. In the center of this boundless chamber stood a round table, carved of light itself. Around it sat the Gods—radiant figures, yet strangely calm, as though ordinary hosts.

They were sipping tea. One god dipped a biscuit into his cup and nibbled it. Another chuckled at some unheard jest.

Nika gasped, scrambling to her feet, her heart pounding.

The gods turned toward her, their eyes like galaxies, their faces both kind and terrible. One of them, with a voice like the rustle of wind through mountains, spoke gently:

"Ah. The mortal princess awakens. Come, child. Sit. You've earned your place at our table."

"Who are you... and where am I?" Nika whispered, her voice trembling yet curious.

"Do not be afraid of us, child," one of the goddesses said, her tone both soothing and commanding. She extended her hand toward a chair that shimmered into being beside the radiant table. "Sit. Rest."

Nika hesitated only for a moment, then bowed her head humbly and sat down on the chair, her eyes wide as she looked at the glowing figures around her.

"Help yourself," another god said warmly, sliding a plate of golden biscuits towards her. "Drink tea with us, and listen."

"I am the supreme god, Minar," said the tallest of them, his voice echoing like a thousand bells struck at once.

"I am the god of light and warmth, Manul," said a radiant figure, his skin blazing like the surface of the sun.

"I am the goddess of love and feelings, Chaya," spoke a gentle woman clothed in rose-colored light, her eyes kind yet infinite.

"I am the god of particles and matter, Zor," said a massive, broad-shouldered being, his form shifting as if made of sand, stone, and stars at the same time.

"And I," said a calm and commanding voice, "am the goddess of time and space, Lako." She leaned slightly forward, her hair flowing like rivers of starlight, her pupils spiraling galaxies.

Nika could not move, could not even breathe for a moment. Her gaze darted from one god to the next. She did not question them—she felt instinctively that every word they spoke was truth.

"So," Zor began, his voice deep as the earth itself, "before you were born, we had problems with the human race... as always."

Minar's golden face darkened with sorrow.

"We helped humans since their first steps. We stood at the origins of their growth, guided them, whispered ideas into their dreams, gave them fire, music, healing, wisdom. We watched over their spiritual and growth moral. And yet..." he sighed, "...people are such strange creatures. At first, they build, create beauty, strive toward the light... and then, just as quickly, they ruin everything. They destroy what they've made, they burn forests, they enslave, they kill. And this cycle repeats... from one civilization to the next."

Chaya lowered her head, sorrow in her radiant eyes.

"They were given magical allies to help them. Elves... fairies... dragons. But mortals twisted these gifts. Elves were hunted, enslaved, slaughtered."

"So," Lako continued, "we moved the elves behind the waterfalls, into a parallel world where mortals could not reach them. The fairies could no longer hide in forests—mortals set them on fire. We lifted them into the clouds. Dragons burrowed beneath the earth, away from human cruelty. Atlantis, once open to the world, we veiled inside the Bermuda Triangle, so no mortal eyes would find it."

"But even with all this," Manul said, his warm voice stern now, "our efforts were in vain. Humans repeated the same mistakes."

Zor clenched his shifting fists.

"So, we decided: the world needed a bridge. Someone of human blood, but carrying a spark of the divine. A soul of light trapped inside mortal flesh. A guardian."

"And so," Minar said with quiet weight, "we created you, Nika."

Her breath caught in her throat. "Me?"

"At first," Lako said, "we thought to make you only a protector, a soldier. But we changed our minds."

"Yes," Zor agreed, "instead, we would let you live freely. To make your own choices. To prove what a mortal soul mixed with divine essence would do if left to wander, to love, to suffer, and to grow."

Nika's voice quivered. "That's... why I have so many abilities?"

Chaya smiled gently. "Yes. You thought elves gave you magic. You thought dragons, kings, and fairies granted it. But in truth, it was always us. You only wore their gifts like cloaks, but the fire underneath was your own."

Zor leaned closer, his face made of swirling stone.

"You thought the King of Atlantis gave you the magic of water. It was I who did that."

Minar added gravely: "And we even gave you and your friends false memories, so that your journey would seem real to you. Otherwise, you would not have believed in yourself. You needed the test."

Nika's eyes widened. Her heart pounded. "Then why... why do I feel so weak sometimes? Why do I tire so quickly, if all this power is mine?"

For a moment, all the gods were silent. Then Chaya laughed softly, the sound like silver bells.

"Because, dear child, you have been using your gifts at half strength. Your divine spark—the particle of God we placed inside you—has never been awakened. You have lived and fought only as a mortal with borrowed strength. And still you came this far."

Nika's lip trembled. Her mind raced back to her friends.

"The mirrored rooms... my friends. They were trapped. Ios... Ios is dead. Was it all a dream? Did I even get out? Or am I still inside?"

Manul leaned forward, his blazing eyes steady.

"No dream. You passed the test. You emerged because your heart is full of love, and your soul is pure. The others fight their battles still. Some may fail, some may rise. Each must face themselves."

"You are ready now," Minar said.

"Ready? For what?" she asked, her voice barely more than a whisper.

"For the awakening," Lako said simply.

And before Nika could speak, before she could ask another question, the chamber of light dissolved. The gods, the table, the endless white floor—all vanished like smoke.

She gasped and found herself once again in the cold, familiar cave in Tibet. Around her, the faces of her friends: Lorenzo, Santigo, Lucas, Alex, Taria. And there—on the stone floor—the lifeless body of Ios.

"What was that?" Lorenzo exclaimed.

"Was it a dream, or was it real?" Lucas muttered, looking pale.

"I remember very well," Taria said softly. "We entered the temple, and then... we were swallowed by mirrors. That much is true."

Chapter 57: Epilogue

"My friends... oh, how glad I am to see you all again." Nika's voice trembled as if her heart could not hold all the wonder inside. Her eyes shone, reflecting the endless ocean sky above them. "It wasn't a dream. No—how could it be? We all dreamed the same dream, lived the same danger. It can't be coincidence. We really were in the Temple of the Seven Seas."

The others stood in a silent circle, the salt wind tangling their hair, their clothes still torn from battle, their faces pale but alive. Lorenzo leaned on his sword like a cane, his sharp eyes watching her, but softer now. Lucas's usual restlessness was gone, replaced by awe. Taria clasped her hands to her chest, her lips whispering silent prayers of gratitude. Alex squinted against the sun, trying to hide the emotion in his eyes. Even Santigo, always skeptical, crossed himself under his breath.

But Nika's gaze was fixed on the figure lying motionless on the deck.

Ios.

He looked as though he slept, but too still, too pale, as though the sea itself had drained the warmth from his body.

"My friends," Nika whispered, kneeling beside him. "I must fix something... I cannot let this end like this."

She lowered herself onto her shins, the wooden deck rough beneath her knees. Her hands trembled as she placed them gently on Ios's cold chest. Closing her eyes, she breathed deeply, her lips moving with words too quiet for the wind.

"I believe... I believe... I believe, and I really want to..."

Her voice cracked, but she pressed on, pouring her whole soul into those fragile syllables.

Behind her, Taria seemed to understand without words. She stepped forward, her silken Atlantean robe brushing the deck as she knelt behind Nika. Placing her hands firmly on Nika's shoulders, she too began to whisper:

"I believe. I believe. I believe..."

One by one, the others followed. Lorenzo, grumbling at sentiment yet drawn in by something larger than pride, placed his hands on Taria's shoulders. Lucas rested his hands on Lorenzo's. Alex, hesitant only a moment, placed his hands on Lucas's shoulders. Finally, Santigo, the doubter, the wanderer, the one who dreamed of

Spain, joined last. His weathered hands landed on Alex's shoulders, completing the chain.

A circle of faith.

"Whatever you do, Nika", Taria thought fiercely, "we believe in you."

And then—something shifted.

A warmth stirred deep inside Nika, spreading through her veins like molten light. She gasped, but did not let go. The warmth grew, and with it an energy so vast it could scarcely be contained. It was not just hers; it flowed through her from all of them—from Taria, from Lorenzo, from Lucas, from Alex, even from Santigo. The chain was alive.

Her body blazed with light. Not gold, not silver—green, the color of rebirth, of spring leaves after winter, of the deep ocean before dawn.

The glow spilled over Ios. His chest rose sharply. Air rushed into his lungs as though the sea itself had breathed into him.

His eyes flew open.

At first he saw nothing—only dazzling light, then shadows, then the blurred outlines of faces leaning over him. For a moment he thought he was still lost in the dream-world of the Temple. He remembered the silence there, the vastness, the feeling of drifting between worlds. He remembered thinking of his friends, of battles left unfinished, of words he had never spoken. He had been so cold, so tired... and yet he had heard something. Voices, faint but insistent, calling him back. I believe... I believe...

And then, with a shudder, life returned.

"What happened? Where am I?" His voice was harsh but alive.

Tears burst from Nika's eyes. She threw her arms around him, holding him as though she would never let go. "You just slept for a long time, my brother. And now you are awake."

The others crowded around, laughter and relief spilling out all at once. Lorenzo thumped him on the back so hard he nearly knocked him flat again. Lucas, unable to hide his joy, shouted, "By Zeus, you had us thinking you were gone forever!"

Even Santigo, normally restrained, bent down and muttered, "Welcome back, chico. Don't scare us like that again."

And Nika—still clinging to him—began to tell the tale. She spoke of the Temple, of her trial, of the gods who tested her, of the moment she nearly lost hope but found it again in their names. Her words tumbled out like a tide, and the crew listened as though hearing prophecy.

When she finished, silence reigned for a breath. Then Lorenzo, his eyes glinting, stepped closer. Without hesitation, he slide his arms around her waist, pulling her gently to him. The world fell away; even the sea seemed to hush.

"You never cease to amaze me," he murmured, and kissed her.

The kiss was soft, reverent, almost disbelieving. The others pretended not to stare, though Alex smirked, and Taria hid a smile.

When at last Nika pulled back, her cheeks flushed, she pressed a hand to Lorenzo's chest and laughed shakily. "Wait, captain. Don't think you can distract me with this. We still have unfinished finished business."

"What business?" asked Lucas, grinning.

"A new adventure," Nika declared. Her voice rank with energy, daring the world to challenge her. "Who is with me?"

The crew exchanged glances. Then, with one voice, they shouted:

"We are with you!"

"We are with you even to the ends of the world!" Taria added, her eyes blazing with loyalty.

"Well then," Nika said, lifting her hand. "Let's go."

In a flash of light, she teleported them.

They landed on the deck of an empty ship, its sails furled, its timbers creaming as though it had been waiting for them all along. The air smelled of salt and pine, and the sea rocked it gently like a cradle.

"Whose ship is this?" Alex asked, eyes wide.

"Now," Nika said with a mischievous smile, "it is ours."

The wind caught the sails as though in answer.

"And we," Nika continued, "will be a new crew. A family. A legend. We shall be known as..."

She hesitated, but before she could speak, the others cried in unison:

"The White Ghost!"

The name echoed across the sea like a vow.

But not all questions were answered. Taria, always sharp, tilted her head. "Nika, you said unfinished business. What business is that?"

Nika smiled and walked to the stern. She whistled, a high, piercing sound that only the sea could hear.

Moments later, the water broke, and a sleek gray dolphin leapt high into the air before landing with a splash beside the ship. He chirped, squeaked, and circled the hull.

"Zack," Nika whispered.

She held out her hands. Magic shimmered from her palms, and with a gentle motion she lifted him from the sea itself, placing him on the deck. His eyes met hers, filled with ancient knowledge.

"Hi, brother," she squeaked in the dolphin's tongue. "Do you want to join us?"

"I would love to," the dolphin squeaked back. "But how could I?"

"Like this."

She touched his sleek head. Light spread, wrapping him in waves of green and silver. The form shifted, stretched, reshaped—until a young man stood before them, water dripping from his hair, his sea-glass eyes shining like the deep.

The crew gasped.

Zack staggered, staring at his hands, flexing his fingers with astonishment. "I... I can breathe air. I can walk." He took one step, then another, nearly tripping on the deck planks, and laughed. "It feels so strange. Heavy... but good."

Lucas muttered, "By the gods..." and Alex added, "This is impossible."

"Nothing is impossible," Nika said proudly. "Not when family is involved."

"Lucas, Ios, Alex," she continued, "this is Zack—my brother. Do you remember the dolphin from years ago, the one we saved on the beach? This is him. He is family."

For a moment, none of them spoke. Then Ios, still weak but alive, managed a smile. "Then... welcome, brother. If Nika trusts you, so do we."

Zack's sea-glass eyes glistened. For the first time in his life, he felt not like a creature of two worlds, but like he belonged somewhere.

Much has changed since those days.

The King of Syracuse did not wait for Charles's return. After years of rule, he died, and the queen took his throne. Under her reign the kingdom healed, casting off poverty and misery. The people thrived, no longer pawns in a king's endless games of war.

Taria, after many farewells to her father, her brother, and the whole kingdom of Atlantis, chose to travel with Nika still. "The sea is," wide she said, "and my heart belongs to adventure as much as home."

Santigo, in contrast, could not resist the call of his homeland. He had dreamed of Spain for years, and when the chance came, Nika made his wish real. He returned with sacks of gold, living in clover, happy at last, far from the sea.

Lorenzo stayed with Nika, his heart bound to hers, not just by vows but by the unspoken fire of shared battles and scars. Lucas, Ios, and Alex swore never to leave her side again, and they kept that vow through calm seas and storms alike. Even Zack—still adjusting to life on two legs—laughed at his own clumsy stumbles, his laughter carrying like music over the waves. Every day he grew stronger, steadier, as though the sea itself was teaching him how to walk in this new world.

Together they sailed across endless waters, chasing horizons no map could mark, guided less by charts and more by trust, courage, and the bond they had forged in fire and blood. Some nights they spoke of the future—of kingdoms rebuilt, of homes waiting in distant lands, of new treasures that were not gold or jewels but the kind found in friendship and love. Other nights they were silent, only the stars speaking above, ancient and eternal witnesses to their voyage.

And the gods?

They did not turn away.

From their thrones in the Temple of the Seven Seas and from the hidden palaces of the deep, they watched.

"They are fragile, yet unbreakable," Minar murmured, his eyes reflecting the constellations.

"They are reckless," Chaya countered, though her lips curved with something like pride.

"They are ours," said Manul simply, and even the thunder god bowed his head in agreement.

Thus, the immortals kept their vigil. For they knew that as long as Nika and her crew sailed, the fragile balance between gods and mortals would never again be as it was. Something had shifted, forever.

But their story was not an ending. It was a threshold, a doorway wide as the ocean itself. Behind them lay battles, betrayals, and loss. Ahead stretched a sea of possibility—uncharted, untamed, eternal.

The sea was wide, and adventure endless.

The White Ghost sailed on.

And the world, whether ready or not, would remember her name.

The End.

Afterword –Nika's Voice

"If you ever find yourself staring at the horizon, wondering if you were meant for more—listen.

The sea is calling.

I was once just a girl who dreamed too loudly, who disobeyed her father's rules, who believed stories were more than stories. They told me I was reckless, foolish, even cursed. Perhaps I am all those things. But I have learned this: it is better to be reckless in love and courage than safe in fear.

Heroes are not chosen by crowns, nor by swords, nor even by the gods. Heroes are chosen by the choices they make when no one is watching. And if I can be one—then so can you.

So sail your seas. Fight your storms. Keep your friends close, for they are your true treasure. And when the world calls you weak, or worthless, or lost—laugh, and prove it wrong.

Because the sea is wide, and adventure endless.

And somewhere out there, beneath the same stars, I am still sailing."

— Nika, the White Ghost

Table Of Contents

Part I: The Prophecy Begins

Part II: The Beginning of a Legend

Part VI: Fairies and The Unknown

Part VII: The Temple

Table of Contents..........................210